HOW HEATHCLIFF STOLE CHRISTMAS

NEVERMORE BOOKSHOP MYSTERIES, BOOK 3.5

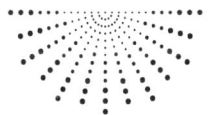

STEFFANIE HOLMES

BACCHANALIA HOUSE

To all the book boyfriends
who keep me up at night.

"A lovely thing about Christmas is that it's compulsory, like a thunderstorm, and we all go through it together."
– Garrison Keillor, *Leaving Home*

CHAPTER ONE

*A*h, Christmas. The most wonderful time of the year. The village streets dusted with freshly fallen snow, the delicious scent of gingerbread and fruit mince pies wafting on the breeze, everyone coming together to rejoice and be kind to their fellow humans—

"… I'm going to rip your arms off and shove them so far up your arse you'll be able to tickle your own tonsils from the inside."

Well, almost everyone.

"You'd better get in there." Quoth rushed into the Children's room, where I was lining the edges of the shelves with strings of tinsel and sparkly baubles, courtesy of my mother's latest pyramid scheme – designer decorations that cost about as much as a small car. "He's about to go full nuclear at Morrie."

It didn't take a rocket scientist to guess who Quoth meant by 'he.' As well as being the world's most swoon-worthy literary anti-hero and a useful member of our amateur murder mystery-solving quartet, Heathcliff Earnshaw owned Nevermore Bookshop. He could also be a world-class grump. I recently learned his grouch-o-meter dialed up to eleven the minute the calendar flipped over to December 1st. What I hadn't yet discovered was *why*. Heathcliff was a soft, cuddly kitten once I'd peeled back all the layers of wanker, but lately, he'd been snapping at me and shooting down all my ideas. It was as if he were putting up all the walls we'd worked so hard to tear down.

I was determined that Heathcliff's temper would be my next mystery to solve. Hopefully, I'd uncover the secret before he took his mounting rage out on an innocent customer.

Not that Morrie was innocent in any way. Nevertheless, I dropped my roll of tinsel and ran into the main room. I paused at the doorway, allowing light from the numerous lamps to reveal the scene.

Heathcliff stood over his desk, his hands balled into fists and his dark skin reddening with rage.

Morrie – short for James Moriarty, the infamous nemesis of Sherlock Holmes – lounged in the velvet armchair in front of the poetry shelves, unconcerned with the rising volcano of Mt. Earnshaw. Beside Morrie sat an old-fashioned boombox pumping out a tinny Christmas carol at top volume.

"No Christmas music in this shop!" Heathcliff boomed. "This is a Christmas-free zone."

"For a Christmas-free zone, things are looking pretty jolly in here. You let Mina put up decorations all over the place," Morrie pointed out without looking up from his book. He didn't have to – strings of tinsel and miniature books sparkled along the edge of Heathcliff's desk, and the oak table sagged under the weight of a large nativity scene with a stable made from books. Morrie and I had been sneakily adding figurines to the display when Heathcliff's back was turned, and it now included a robot Jesus and a wise man carrying a sign that read, JAMES MORIARTY FOR PRIME MINISTER. "*And* you agreed Quoth could erect the Christmas monolith."

To emphasize his point, Morrie reached up and tugged one of the looming branches of Quoth's Christmas tree. Big mistake.

Spruce needles rained down on his head, and a twinkling glass bauble beaned him in the forehead.

Every year, the village of Argleton ran a charity tree for the local animal shelter. A different shop hosted the tree each holiday season, decorating it how they wished and erecting it prominently on their premises. Villagers would drop off donations of cat and dog food, guinea pig cages, toys, pet beds, envelopes of money, and other supplies. They could also leave their names on a list if they were interested in adopting a shelter animal. It was an amazing community project and really helped the animal shelter get through the busy holiday months.

When he wasn't preening, hiding in the attic, or defecating on customers who quoted his titular poem, Quoth volunteered at the animal shelter. Touched by the plight of sick and unwanted animals at Christmas, Quoth offered Nevermore Bookshop to host the charity tree. After much bitching, Heathcliff agreed, provided the tree was 'minuscule and not a bloody nuisance.' Our instructions in hand, Quoth and I went to the King's Copse Wood Christmas Tree lot to pick out our tree, and he fell absolutely in love with a twelve-foot spruce of needly magnificence. What could I say? Clearly not 'no,' since that same tree now dominated the main room of the shop. We'd had to move the Science Fiction bookcase and our leather sofa just to make room in the bay window, and even then branches touched all four walls of the room, obscuring much of the shelving and drooping a needly canopy over Heathcliff's desk. Since the ceiling was only ten feet high, the top branches scraped across the plaster like jolly Lovecraftian tentacles devouring everything in their path.

Heathcliff went postal when he saw it… perhaps with good reason. But he'd promised Quoth and me, so he'd endured the tree's presence in festering silence. The tree wasn't the only thing getting the silent treatment from Heathcliff – he'd barely spoken a word to me in two days, and it was kind of breaking my heart.

Now I faced him across the room as he fought to control the urge to clobber Morrie, and I'd never felt more distant from him.

Why is he so upset over a Christmas song? I wish he'd talk to me instead of lashing out. Morrie can handle him, but Quoth...

"My tree is for *charity*." Quoth stiffened, a note of vexation creeping into his voice. Quoth rarely got angry, preferring to direct his feelings inward. Heathcliff and Morrie walked a dangerous line by picking on Quoth's big, beautiful heart.

"Exactly. Quoth's tree is for the animals. And Mina gets her bloody tinsel and her poxy nativity because she's annoyingly persistent," Heathcliff shot back at Morrie. "And she has lovely breasts. You do not have lovely breasts."

"But I *can* be very annoying." Morrie reached over and turned up the volume knob.

Heathcliff's face glowed even redder. "Get rid of that boombox or it's joining the rest of your limbs up your anus—"

"No can do." Morrie shook needles out of his book and turned the page. "It's my Christmas present for Mina. I got it at the village Christmas market with a whole trunk of old punk cassettes. She's going to love it. I'm just testing it to make sure it works. You wouldn't want me to give Mina a useless gift, would you?"

My heart fluttered at Morrie's words. A vintage boombox and old punk cassettes? That was an *awesome* present.

Which was a big problem. Morrie found me the perfect present. I knew Quoth was making me something, because there was a square of canvas in his room with a sheet over it, and he refused to let me peek underneath. Since he was an amazing artist, I knew whatever he'd created would be beautiful. Heathcliff adamantly claimed he didn't believe in Christmas gifts, but he was acting so strange that I didn't know if he was fibbing. If he was, that meant that all three of my boyfriends put a ton of thought into my Christmas presents.

And I had no idea what to do for them. They were so different that three of the same generic gift wouldn't cut it. Whenever I thought of something that would work for one of them, I struggled with an equivalent idea for the other two. I didn't want one to feel as though he was less favored than the others. This was turning out to be the most stressful Christmas gift-buying experience since I was seven, when my mother joined a cult and declared everything we owned now had to be made of hemp.

Who knew having three boyfriends at Christmastime was so bloody complicated? I can't just…

Oh, no. I tuned back into the scene in front of me. I'd let my thoughts distract me, and now—

Heathcliff had that *look* in his eyes.

The *stabby* look.

My hands raised to protect myself from the overhanging branches, I stepped forward to place myself between the two of them before Heathcliff unleashed a hail of Victorian gothic fury. "Hey guys, it's Christmas. Rule number one on Mina's new Christmas shop rules is no fighting during the holiday season. Morrie, your gift sounds very sweet, but I think you should probably turn it down—"

"No fair. Now you know what I'm getting you." Morrie stuck out his lower lip. "I'm going to have to find something else so it's a surprise."

"That's fine! You don't have to—"

"You heard the woman. I'm turning it off." Heathcliff strode across the room.

"You can't," Morrie piped up.

"Why not?"

"I glued the button down," Morrie grinned, pointing to the top of the box. "This thing is gonna blast Snoopy's Christmas all day and night. You're welcome."

"You're dog meat." Heathcliff's huge hands wrapped around Morrie's throat. Morrie's eyes bugged out of his head in a spot-on imitation of Homer Simpson throttling his son.

The problem was, Morrie wasn't a cartoon character, and he needed air to breathe and kiss me and be his usual annoying self. I grabbed Heathcliff's hands and tried to pry them off. "Heathcliff, let him go. You're hurting him—"

"Oh, how lovely. It's nice to hear Nevermore getting into the spirit of Christmas this year!"

I jumped as Mrs. Ellis shuffled into the room, ushering a sullen-looking girl of about twelve toward the display of young adult books I'd arranged on the room's one unobstructed shelf. Mrs. Ellis admired the snogging wise men in the nativity scene and beamed at us, seemingly not noticing the murder unfolding before her.

Heathcliff dropped Morrie, who slumped forward in relief, clutching his throat. "You saved my life, Mrs. Ellis," he gasped.

"Don't be so bloody dramatic." Heathcliff shuffled back to his chair and slumped down. The sudden movement dislodged a hail of needles on top of him. He glared at the large tote bag slung over Mrs. Ellis' shoulder. "Please tell me you have a flask in there? I'm in desperate need of Christmas cheer."

"Not today, I'm afraid. I'm playing Santa Claus, delivering presents to all my favorite people around the village. The Banned Book Club. The Knobbly Knitters. My Bondage and Discipline for Pensioners circle…" Mrs. Ellis fished around in her bag and drew out a large box wrapped in bright paper, which she handed to the girl. "I brought my granddaughter Jonie around to put a gift under the tree. She's staying with me over the Christmas holidays while my daughter Deirdre is in Paris with her new boyfriend. Jonie loves all kinds of animals. Deirdre doesn't care for them, so Jonie's not allowed a pet of her own, but she's happy to help the animals of Argleton find their forever homes this Christmas."

Jonie didn't look happy to help. In fact, she and Heathcliff could've been twins with their scowling faces and stormy eyes. A pair of brown braids trailed over a sweatshirt, accentuating her long face and gloomy expression. Oblivious to her granddaughter's mood (as she was to many things), Mrs. Ellis shoved Jonie toward me. "Go on, dear. Mina will show you where the tree is."

"You can't bloody miss it, you blind old bint," Heathcliff muttered as I pointed Jonie to the pile of presents dwarfed by the gargantuan conifer.

"Hey!" I slapped his arm. "Don't mock the blind."

Despite his rotten mood, Heathcliff had the decency to look abashed. Even though I was doing a lot better since I learned that I had a rare condition called retinitis pigmentosa, I was still not quite ready to joke about my degrading eyesight.

However, Heathcliff did have a point. The tree *was* hard to miss. I patted a branch, sending a shower of needles across the floor. "You can put the present anywhere you like. We've just started the collection today, but already we've had a few people make their donations." I didn't want to mention in Heathcliff's presence that most of the presents there were from Quoth and me.

Jonie grunted as she bent down and slid her parcel under the tree. She stood up, rubbing her arms. "It's freezing in here."

"Agreed." I shivered as a cold gust of wind whipped past me. Ever since the weather had turned, we've been experiencing random cold drafts in the shop. I'd added draft stoppers to all the windows, but it hadn't helped, and we had no idea where the cold came from. Even spending a small fortune on wood to light fires on both floors hadn't helped warm the place up. "Mrs, Ellis, you should introduce Jonie to Grimalkin and Quoth. I bet she'd love—"

"Mina, dear!" The shop bell tinkled as a familiar voice trilled through the shop. "I've got something amazing to show you."

A moment later, my mother strolled through the door, swinging an enormous tote bag and juggling an armful of colorful wrapping paper rolls. Every inch of her was covered in Christmas bling – from the sparkly elf hat placed at a jaunty angle atop her head to the Christmas fairy pins stuck all over her blouse and the jingle-bell beaded bracelets on her wrists. She looked like a Christmas tree.

"My new range arrived, and it's divine—Oh, Mina, how *could* you?" Mum's voice trembled with hurt as she flung down her supplies, sending wrapping paper and needles flying in all directions. My mouth dropped open as Mum whipped Jonie's present from her hands and started tearing off the paper. "I *told* you I was sponsoring the charity tree. All the presents are supposed to be wrapped in my special Bedazzled Bethlehem papers!"

Bedazzled Bethlehem was the name of Mum's new 'business.' My mother had recently lost her job as a tarot reader at the local New Age shop after one of her DIY soap kits exploded. Luckily, Helen Wilde never let setbacks or cold, hard reality get her down. She'd thrown herself into her latest get-rich-quick scheme – selling overpriced designer Christmas wrapping paper, baubles, and decorations. Unlike many of her other schemes, the products were actually quite nice, but they were ridiculously overpriced and I knew when January rolled around she wouldn't be able to sell a string of tinsel to an elf.

I never should have accepted two boxes of decorations from her to decorate the shop and tree in exchange for leaving a stack of her business cards on the counter. I thought that was what she'd meant by *sponsorship*. Apparently, she had much more dramatic plans.

"What are you doing to my present?" Jonie demanded, thrusting her hands on her hips.

I grabbed the box from Mum and tried to stick the tape back down. "Mum, you can't expect everyone to use your products. Sponsorship means you donate the wrapping paper. If that's what you're doing, then—"

"Heavens no, I can't afford that!" Mum started to pull more rolls of fancy foil paper and sparkly ribbons from her tote. "I know! I'll set up a gift-wrapping table. Customers can pay me to wrap their gifts for them, and peruse my stock at the same time!"

Inwardly, I groaned. Maybe Heathcliff was onto something with that stiff drink. "It's a lovely idea, Mum, but I'm afraid we don't have room for a gift-wrapping table—"

"Nonsense. It won't be in your way at all." Mum swept a stack of books off the corner of Heathcliff's desk. "I'll set up right here, so the customers can see me as soon as they come in."

Heathcliff boomed. "Now, just a minute there, Mrs. Wilde. No one touches *my* desk—"

"I've even got a present to wrap to show them how it's done." Ignoring Heathcliff's protests, Mum whipped out a glass bottle with a spray top. "This is a catnip extract. Sylvia Blume makes it. You simply spritz it around and it helps your cat feel calm and playful."

She started to spray the rug in front of the desk. A foul smell – like damp newspaper and petrol fumes – assailed my nostrils. Mrs. Ellis pinched her nose. Jonie made a face.

"Meeeeeow!" Grimalkin somersaulted through the air, landing on the rug and rolling around in the spray like a drug addict relishing the first hit.

"See?" Mum beamed. She set the bottle on the counter and rolled out a paper covered in foil reindeer. "Now, to wrap an unusually-shaped present like this, you want to fold this edge down and crimp it—"

"There will be no crimping on my desk!" Heathcliff boomed.

"Merry Christmas." A bespeckled face peered around the door. Our accountant, Bertie Robinson, stepped gingerly over the threshold. Bertie had been doing the store accounts for the previous owner, Mr. Simson, since practically the beginning of time. After Mr. Simson disappeared, Heathcliff had kept Bertie on – he acted as a stoic and sensible voice to counter Heathcliff's impassioned moods. Bertie wore his trademark black suit – the shoulders dusted with snow – and a grey tie decorated with holly leaves. It was the most festive I'd ever seen him. "Mina, Heath-cliff, I've come to start on the accounts."

I raised an eyebrow in surprise. Bertie popped in to collect our ledger on the 25th of the month at 2PM. You could set your watch by him. He was three days and five hours early. *What's going on?*

"I apologize for being early, but I did send an email," Bertie stammered, sensing my unease.

"I didn't read it," Heathcliff muttered.

"I'm trying to get a jump on things before the holidays and… well, my wife lost her job at the Post Office and I've seven hungry mouths to feed and I could really use the money."

"You have seven children?" Morrie looked appalled. "You should be institutionalized."

Bertie shook his head as he stepped over Grimalkin, who was still wallowing in her catnip-soaked paradise. "Princess – that's our golden retriever – gave birth to five in October. We didn't even know she was pregnant. The puppies need special food and vet checkups, and with Elizabeth out of work, we just can't afford it. That's why I was hoping I could do the store accounts early, and maybe get my invoice paid on time for once."

Bertie looked like a defenseless puppy himself, perched in the doorway with wide, hopeful eyes. I thought of the receipts and unpaid invoices strewn across the office. I'd tried to start the accounts yesterday but I'd misplaced my favorite sparkly pen and by the time I'd hunted all over for it, Heathcliff was yelling about the display of Christmas storybooks I'd made in the front hall and I had to appease him.

"I'm afraid things are a bit of a mess," I said.

Bertie's face perked up. "You know, I've been meaning to talk to you, Mina. It would make your life so much easier if you switched to an online system. You'd be able to reconcile accounts and see data in real-time, and—"

"No, I don't want it," Jonie yelled.

I whirled around in time to see Mum drape a tinsel garland around Jonie's neck. Tiny dog ornaments wearing Santa hats dangled from the tinsel. As Jonie twisted to try and free herself, Mum wound the end around her body, wrapping her up like a Christmas mummy.

"This is my range for animal lovers," Mum explained over Jonie's protests. "I've got matching greeting card sets and advent calendars and—"

"Heathcliff will help you, Bertie," I called as I tried to help Jonie untangle herself from the tinsel. "He owns the shop, so he's the one you have to talk to about cloud accounting."

Bertie visibly stiffened. "Oh, no, I wouldn't want to bother him. I'll come back later, when you're free. I'm sure Heathcliff is very busy—"

"I'm right here, Bertie," Heathcliff bellowed. "And today of all days, I'd be happy to talk about the accounts. Step into my office."

Bertie shuddered. "Last time I did that you slammed my fingers in the ledger."

"You can't still be harping on about that."

"Just a moment, Heathcliff." Mum stepped toward him, brandishing an enormous Santa hat bedecked in red glitter. "I got this for you. I was thinking you'd be perfect to play Santa for the kids at the housing estate youth center this year—"

"Accounts. Now." Heathcliff grabbed Bertie's shoulder and dragged him into the office, slamming the door behind him and leaving Mum dangling a Santa hat in midair.

"Croak!" Quoth had reappeared in his raven form on top of the door. He flapped his wings to draw my attention to some new customers.

"Meow!" That was Grimalkin prancing across Heathcliff's desk, butting the catnip spray bottle over the edge.

"Oh, no you don't." I lunged and managed to catch the bottle before it could smash on the floor. Grimalkin shot me a filthy look and flopped over onto her back.

"Have we come at a bad time?" A mother and child, holding a stack of wrapped gifts, stood in front of the poetry shelves. "We just wanted to leave our gifts for the animals."

"No, no, come on in." As I ushered them toward the tree, I noticed more people in the hall behind them. I mouthed to Morrie to deal with my mother and the bloody cat, plastered on my best customer service smile, and went out to speak to my customers. Self-consciously, I touched my hand to my hair. I'd tried to create a festive look by pinning a string of tinsel through my hair, but several of my sparkly bobby pins had disappeared, so my 'do kept drooping.

"Look at these lovely Christmas storybooks!" a woman cooed, picking one up from the display.

"And these leatherbound editions." A man wearing a hideous Christmas sweater peered at a set of the complete works of Jane Austen. "This is the perfect gift for my wife."

"These decorations are lovely." Cynthia Lachlan fingered the strings of tinsel I'd used to line the bookshelves in the hall. "I must get some for Lachlan House. It's great to see Nevermore Bookshop finally embracing the Christmas spirit."

I glowed with their praise. Ever since I started working here, I'd wanted everyone in Argleton to realize Nevermore Bookshop was special and magical, and that its surly proprietor was actually a big soft teddy bear on the inside. If I could make the first thing happen, then surely the second was right around the corner?

The gifts piled up under the tree as more and more villagers filed into the shop. Morrie managed to wrangle my mother into working the ancient till, and she chatted merrily with customers as she upsold them on expensive wrapping paper and 'Bedazzled Gift Caddies,' whatever those were. Quoth perched on Morrie's shoulder, tugging books from the shelves with his beak and handing them to customers while Morrie talked up the merits of giving the gift of reading this Christmas. Heathcliff and Bertie remained locked in the office, which was probably for the best since I'd never seen the shop this full. Grimalkin was still wriggling on the catnip-soaked rug. My stomach flipped in a giddy, happy dance.

As I helped a little boy find a place under the tree, Tabitha O'Shea walked in. Tabitha was a posh friend of Cynthia Lachlan, and she looked the part today in a figure-hugging coat of fine cashmere, leather trousers, and Louboutin heels. Her husband was a diplomat and was usually overseas on business, so Tabitha filled her time by sinking her perfectly-manicured nails into a million community projects (and also, according to Mrs. Ellis, several of the community's eligible bachelors). She volunteered at the housing estate youth center with Mum as well as at the animal shelter with Quoth, and she was also responsible for organizing the charity tree every year. "Mina, I can't tell you how happy we are that you're in charge of the charity tree this year." Tabitha beamed, clutching my hands as she gazed at the mounting present stack and majestic tree in awe. "Nevermore Bookshop has never participated before, but I can already see this will be the best tree yet. Those animals are going to be so spoiled thanks to the town's generosity."

"Thanks. I was worried the tree was a little too big, but everyone seems to be loving it."

"Nonsense. A Christmas tree can never be too big, and yours is simply majestic!" She circled the tree – well, as much of the tree as one could circle without crashing into a wall – and fingered Mum's glitzy baubles. "And those decorations! They're absolutely stunning. It's a Christmas wonderland in here. It will be the perfect location for the calendar photo shoot!"

"The... what?"

"Didn't I tell you?" Her eyes sparkled. "Every year the village puts together a charity calendar for the New Year. Local personalities are the models for each month, and we pose them in front of the charity tree or with different Christmas-themed props. All the businesses contribute props and logo-ed G-strings. It's all good, harmless fun. We've booked the shoot. We've got a famous photographer coming all the way from London – Roland Crabapple."

"Roland *Crabapple* is shooting the Christmas calendar?" I nearly choked. I knew his work from my fashion industry days. He was famous for shooting the more... shall we say, *risqué* editorials and celebrity BDSM parties. "Is this calendar going to be... PG?"

"Oh, of course, of course! Just a little bare chest, maybe a few cheeky cheeks. A little something to titillate the Argleton housewives." Tabitha glanced around the room, her eyes resting on my mother behind the desk. "I was actually wondering if I could talk to Mr. Heathcliff. I thought he'd like to model—"

"HELL NO!" Heathcliff bellowed from behind the closed office door.

How did he hear her? Heathcliff must have supersonic hearing when it came to people suggesting his involvement in Christmas community events.

"Don't mind him." Morrie materialized at my side, grinning that dangerously sexy smile of his. "Heathcliff may be one hot piece of ass, but he's basically the sexy Grinch who stole Christmas. He's the last person you'd want on your calendar. I, on the other hand, would be happy to assist..."

Tabitha looked Morrie up and down, biting her lower lip in barely-concealed lust. What Morrie lacked in Heathcliff's imposing bulk and muscle, he more than made up with his impressive height, wiry muscles tense with excited energy, and those glacier eyes that seemed to strip any woman bare.

"Oh, that's wonderful," Tabitha purred. "And who are you?"

"James Moriarty, at your service." Morrie took a deep bow. "I'm Heathcliff's flatmate, and the only thing I like more than taking my clothes off for a good cause is making sure I do everything I can to be on Santa's naughty list."

"Oh, yes. You'll do nicely." Tabitha ran her manicured nails along Morrie's arm. "I'm sure I must've mentioned the shoot to you, Mina. It's all been arranged. Roland's booked to come up from London, and he wants to start the shoot day after tomorrow at 7AM sharp to capture the early morning light. That means we'll have to be at the shop at 5AM to set up the lights and get everything ready." Her shoulders sagged. "Oh, no. That's really too early to ask you to accommodate us when your friends live upstairs."

"Kinda, yeah." My eyes flicked to the closed office door. 5AM? Not bloody likely. Not Christmas Eve, the morning after the village Christmas market. I planned to get very drunk on hot toddies, stay over at the bookshop, and shag my boyfriends all night.

Morrie gestured to his body. "Sorry, luv. All of *this* needs eight hours solid shut-eye."

Tabitha lowered her gaze. "Forget I said anything. We'll find another location for the shoot. Perhaps Richard over at the Rose & Wimple pub will let us use the pool room—"

An idea occurred to me. "Not to worry." I dug into my pocket and produced my shop key. "I'll give you this. It unlocks the front door. Just let yourselves in and do what you have to do, then return it to me when we drag ourselves out of bed."

Tabitha's face brightened. "Are you sure? We won't disturb you?"

"Nah, we sleep pretty soundly." *Especially after all the alcohol and shagging.*

She eyed the table with the nativity scene. "Can we move a few things around? Roland will love the tree – he's obsessed with foliage, but he'll want to get the lighting just right. Even with all the lamps, it's a very dark shop."

"Don't I know it." Even with the lamps blazing all day, I still tripped over things and banged into shelves. "Sure. Just put everything back before you leave. Bring some tape to make a

.

note of the furniture alignment, because if the table is even a few inches from where it should be..."

Tabitha's gaze settled on Heathcliff's locked office door. She gulped. "I promise. Thank you, Mina. It means a lot to me, and the village, how much you've turned this shop around."

A lump rose in my throat. I came back to Argleton in a cloud of shame and depression after I got my diagnosis and lost my amazing fashion industry job. I felt like a failure, and I'd wanted so bad to prove that I could make a success of *something* in my life. To know that the work I'd done at Nevermore had been noticed and appreciated made me choke up. "That means a lot. I honestly thought I'd hate being back in Argleton, but actually it's —Grimalkin, *no!*"

I leaped across the room, my fingers narrowly missing Grimalkin as she scrambled up the tree. The bloody cat tore off with the string of tinsel and flung herself through the air like a bungee jumper. Customers scrambled out of the way as Grimalkin landed on her feet on the rug and took off into the stacks, dragging the tinsel behind her.

"That catnip has made her crazy." I ducked into the stacks just as Grimalkin shot up the side of a bookcase.

"Croak!" Quoth swooped the cat and grabbed the other end of the tinsel. Grimalkin dropped to the floor, rolled over onto her stomach, and kicked at the tinsel with all four paws. Sparkly paper flew in all directions.

"Mina, they're ruining the decorations!" Mum cried.

"Naughty kitty. You don't play with that." I risked life and limb to claim the tinsel back from Grimalkin. "There are plenty of other cat toys around the place. Find one of those."

"Meow!" Grimalkin shot me a glare. She leaped into the air, landing spread-eagled in the tree, which teetered on its stand. I lunged, but I wasn't fast enough. A gasp rose from my throat as the tree toppled sideways, just as Heathcliff stepped out his office door. Tinsel and needles and large glass baubles battered his head as he struggled to hold the weight.

"I hate this bloody tree," Heathcliff growled, his eyes flashing. "I wish we'd never agreed to do this stupid charity thing. Let someone else be the Christmas elf so I can drink in peace. What the *fuck* are all these people doing in my shop?"

Silence fell.

"Sorry, folks." I plastered a smile on my face. "Heathcliff is just kidding. Of course he—"

"I'm not kidding." Heathcliff's face was a storm. "I *hate* Christmas! I wish it didn't exist!"

The children's faces fell. Their mother shot Heathcliff a reproachful look and ushered them away. Tabitha shook her head sadly and tsked under her breath. Jonie looked like she didn't know whether to applaud or run for her life. Mum tried to recover herself by explaining the decorations could be used all year round to 'create a disco effect in your living room.'

Ah, Christmas. The most wonderful time of the year.

CHAPTER TWO

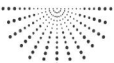

"*I*s Heathcliff like this every year?" I asked Quoth as I watched him swirl his brush in red paint and dab it on the canvas. He'd turned the painting away from me and banished me to one corner of the room so I had no chance of seeing the image, which made my anxiety about finding his perfect Christmas gift *so much better*.

Not.

"He's usually worse." Quoth didn't look up from the canvas. "He never allows decorations in the shop, and he barks at anyone who says Merry Christmas or hums 'Jingle Bells.' It shows how much he cares about you that he let us put that tree up in the first place."

"Well… he didn't so much *let* us put it up," I smiled, remembering. "Morrie and I erected it while he was passed out drunk."

"I wish it didn't have to be like that." Quoth looked away. "I wish he wanted to help the animals, and he didn't just agree to make you happy."

"I'm sure he doesn't mean to upset you."

"He does," Quoth didn't turn around. "Thank you for sticking up to him, Mina. It means a lot to be running the charity tree. I

19

meet all kinds of animals at the shelter, and their stories make me so sad. It gets worse every holiday. Do you know how many people give pets as Christmas presents to family members who aren't ready for them? It's horrible. And then the animal gets neglected and abandoned and it's not their fault…"

Quoth shook his head. His shoulders shuddered. Blatantly ignoring his rule of staying on my side of the canvas, I went over and wrapped my arms around him, pulling him close and breathing in his earthy chocolate and fresh herbs scent. Quoth still struggled with his place in the world – he wasn't entirely human, and yet he wasn't just a bird, either. He was so much more. To me, he was special and unique and wonderful, but when he looked at himself, he didn't see that. He saw a freak who had to hide away. Being involved with the animal shelter was one small step toward Quoth being happy in his own skin.

I knew running this tree meant the world to him – it wasn't just about saving neglected animals. It was about showing in a small way that he was part of the village. That he didn't want to hide away anymore. That he considered this his home enough to put down roots here.

Quoth burrowed his head into my shoulder. Although I itched to peek over Quoth's shoulder at the canvas, I didn't want to ruin his surprise. I tipped his head back and kissed him – using my lips and body to speak my feelings for him because it was Christmas and Quoth was beautiful. He was *my* family. He didn't have to be alone.

Quoth melted into me. Paint-covered fingers grazed my cheek, featherlight and reverent. Warm lips brushed mine, tentative but laced with need.

We slid together, our bodies drawn to each other like punk rockers to safety pins. Quoth kissed with his eyes open – those dark orbs of his boring into me as if he were trying to commit every moment of us to memory.

I planned to give him something to remember.

I nudged Quoth toward the bed, flicking open the buttons on his shirt. I pressed my palm against his chest, feeling his heart pound beneath his skin. Somehow, inside him existed bird parts and human parts all meshed together. He shouldn't exist, and yet he was here, flesh and bone made real and wonderful. He was a miracle.

My miracle.

Our kisses deepened as we tossed away our clothes. I wanted to fall into him, to become part of the miracle of his body. Quoth's fingers trailed down my spine, sending a delicious shiver through my body that had nothing to do with that poxy draft blowing through the attic.

Quoth trailed kisses along my neck, over my collarbone, touching the spot on my clavicle that made me shudder with desire. I reached between his legs and grabbed his cock, stroking it between my fingers. His shoulders tightened and a small sigh escaped his lips.

"Well, well, it looks like our little birdie's stocking is *hung*."

Quoth tore away from me. He scrambled against the wall, his eyes wide as saucers and a scattering of black feathers poking through his cheeks. I whirled around, too wrapped up in the moment to think to be ashamed of my nakedness.

Morrie leaned against the doorframe, a dark smile playing across his lips. "If you keep swinging on Quoth's North Pole like that, you'll be going on Santa's naughty list."

I threw my shirt at him. "You're not funny."

"I am hilarious. Mind if I join you?"

I wanted to protest, to say that tonight should be all about Quoth, but Morrie was already climbing into bed on the other side of me. He tipped my head toward him and claimed my mouth in a hot, needy kiss. It was all I could do not to swoon right there.

James Moriarty had a way of crushing my will with his sexiness. By Isis, the guy knew how to make a woman's body sing, and he pulled out all his tricks – he wanted to stay, and he was determined to earn his place in Quoth's bed.

"Where's Heathcliff?" I murmured. I didn't think it was fair he should miss out.

"He's gone over to the pub to drown his Christmas-induced sorrows." Morrie cupped my cheek to claim my lips. "Although Ishtar knows why he'd do that since it's quiz night tonight."

That *did* seem odd. The Rose & Wimple quiz night would have the whole town crowded into the pub, yelling out answers and trash-talking the other teams and spreading Christmas cheer. It seemed like the last place Heathcliff would want to go. But then Quoth pressed his lips to that spot on my clavicle again and I forgot all about quiz night.

Morrie's tongue danced across mine as Quoth ran the tips of his fingers over my skin, raising trails of goosebumps he kissed into submission. I sank back into Quoth's arms with a sigh as Morrie drew away before closing his lips around my nipple.

I gasped in pleasure as Morrie swirled his tongue around it before scraping his teeth over the sensitive bud. A jolt of desire shot through my body. I gripped Morrie's arm as he bent his head to the other nipple, while Quoth's fingers trailed between my legs.

"Lie back, gorgeous," Morrie whispered. "Tonight, Quoth and I will have you walking in an orgasm wonderland."

If you insist. As I settled back on the pillows, a whoosh of cold air blasted over us. I yelped in surprise. *That bloody draft!*

Quoth pulled the blankets over us, wrapping his arms around my body. Warmth flooded my limbs – from his body heat but also from our closeness, from what we shared now, here, tonight. Quoth's dark eyes swam with love and reverence as he bent his head between my legs.

His tongue dived for my clit, making slow circles that sent me wild. Morrie pinched my nipple between his fingers and flicked his tongue over my lips, smiling that cheeky grin of his as he promised so much more to come.

Heat rose inside me, spreading along my veins until I sizzled with fire and need. Quoth pushed a finger into me as he pressed his tongue against me. Morrie scraped my nipple with his teeth once more, and the heat inside me bubbled over.

My body rocked as an orgasm rippled through me, languid like the ebb of a river dancing over wind-tossed pebbles.

When I rose through the river, Quoth bent over me, a perfect smile grazing his lips. I reached out and gripped his arm, dragging him on top of me and wrapping my legs around him. Quoth let out a whimper as he entered me, a sound so tender and beautiful it broke my heart. His breath warmed my earlobe. Morrie's tongue entwined in mine as he lent his body heat to our embrace.

Quoth's strokes were languid too – he breathed slowly, his gaze falling on mine, his fingers twining in my hair. He opened me like a flower in spring, those eyes and that heart breaking apart the winter ice that had settled on my mind ever since my diagnosis.

We fell into each other – his eyes swallowing those dark parts of me and leaving me with only the light of his love. A second orgasm built inside me, and this one rose like a wild animal and slammed into me, knocking me back against the pillows as my body yielded to Quoth's. He came at the same time, his lip trembling as he rocked against me in deferential bliss.

"Looks like Santa Claus isn't the only one coming to town," Morrie whispered in my ear.

I shoved Morrie. He fell back against the pillows, his hands folded behind his head and that cheeky smirk on his lips. Quoth rolled aside. I climbed onto Morrie and thrust myself down on his cock, moaning a little as my body stretched and shifted to accommodate his girth.

I mashed my mouth against Morrie's, mostly so he'd shut the fuck up.

Morrie groaned as I slammed my pelvis down on him. Tonight, Quoth had my heart, but Morrie held a part of me, too. He drew out something wild and powerful inside me. My last name wasn't Wilde for nothing, and with Morrie, I'd never felt more free, or more bold. The two of them watched me with admiration as I took what I wanted.

I loved this. Being with my three boyfriends made me feel powerful, invincible. It didn't matter that I was going blind. Who cares? I'd rock it, just like I was rocking Morrie's world right now.

"You're smiling." Morrie's nails dug into my hips as he thrust up to meet me. "Does it make you happy, jingling my bells?"

"Maybe." I smiled even wider as I ground against him. Morrie's jaw clenched. His muscles stiffened. I reached behind him, slipping my hand between his legs and scraping my nail down that sensitive stretch of skin between his balls and anus.

"Deck the balls…" I whisper-sung in his ear. Morrie burst out laughing as he came, sending a spasm through his body and causing him to break down into a coughing fit.

We collapsed together, laughing and hugging, pressing our bodies close as another blast of cold air scoured the room. Quoth nuzzled into my shoulder, resting his ear on my chest. Morrie wrapped his arms around both of us, his lips brushing the top of my head. Somewhere downstairs, the building creaked in protest.

The bells at the front door tinkled. *That must be Heathcliff, home from the pub. I wonder if he drank himself into a better mood…*

Beside me, Morrie grabbed his phone from Quoth's night-stand and started scrolling and tapping. I craned my neck to see what he was doing, but he angled his phone away.

"No peeking. I'm planning a Christmas surprise the likes of which you've never encountered before."

"But you already got me an amazing Christmas present. Those cassette tapes—"

"Oh, those are for you to enjoy now. At top volume. While

Heathcliff is nearby." Morrie grinned, kissing my cheek. "Call it a pre-Christmas Christmas gift. I've come up with something even better for the big event."

I flopped back onto the pillow and groaned. Great. Now not only did I have to come up with three epic Christmas gifts, but I had to sort pre-Christmas Christmas gifts, too?

~

*W*hen I opened my eyes again, grey light streamed through the window, casting a square across the narrow bed. I slid out from under Morrie's arm and crept to the window, watching tiny flecks of white tumble through the air.

Snow!

We'd already had a snowfall earlier in the week, but Heathcliff had me doing stocktake in the storage room and I missed it. Well, I wasn't going to miss this one. I stuck my head out the window and breathed in the crisp, wintery scent. Snowflakes dotted my face, collecting in my hair and—

"Who let that draft in?" Morrie muttered, tugging the covers over his naked arse cheeks.

I jumped on the bed, jolting the two of them awake. Quoth tried to drag me down under the covers again, but I wasn't having it.

"It's snowing!" I poked Morrie's ribs. "Let's make snow angels. Let's build a snowman and dress him up like a hipster. Oooh, we need to have a snowball fight…"

"Or… here's an idea." Morrie held up one finger. "You could come back to bed and Quoth and I will make your sleigh bells ring."

I yanked the pillow from under his head and thumped him with it. "Get up. That's an order. Heathcliff! I don't care how hungover you are, it's time to wake up!"

I untangled myself from Morrie and Quoth and scrambled for

my clothes. I hopped across the floor, dragging my fleece leggings over my arse and pulling on Quoth's Blood Lust hoodie over my own for extra warmth. Morrie lunged for me again, but I slipped past him and barreled down the steep attic steps.

"Heathcliff, get up! It's snowing! We're going to have a snow-ball fight, and I demand that you join us. You can work out some of that pent-up Christmas aggression with—yeeeeow!"

My foot landed on a silvery bauble at the bottom of the stairs. My ankle rolled out from under me.

CRASH. I went down in a heap. My knee smashed into Heath-cliff's door.

"Owie," I moaned, clutching my knee. Grimalkin poked her head around the corner of the living room.

"Meow?"

"Yeah, yeah," I muttered, leaning against the wall as I rolled up the hem of my leggings to inspect the bruise already blossoming across my knee.

"Mina, are you okay?" Footsteps clattered down the stairs. Quoth dropped down beside me, his eyes wide. Behind him, Heathcliff's door swung open. A shaft of light pooled across the hallway rug, only to be obscured a moment later by a heavy shadow. Heathcliff loomed over me, wearing the same clothes and coat he had on yesterday, his wild hair rumpled and a pillow crease on his cheek. He narrowed his eyes at the bauble in my hand.

"What's that doing up here?" he demanded. "We agreed – no Christmas decorations in the flat."

"I didn't bring it up here." I flipped the bauble over, noticing my mother's Bedazzled Bethlehem tag stuck to the back. "This is one of the decorations from the tree. It might've got snagged on our clothing last night. Look – there's a bit of black fur stuck under the string." I held up the bauble against the trim on Heath-cliff's rumpled coat, noticing as I did the strong aroma of beer.

"True," Heathcliff grumbled. "I think I did crash into that

bloody tree last night. Mystery solved. Now, I have a date with my morning whisky and—"

I yanked him toward the stairs. "Come on, Mopey McGee. We're having a snowball fight whether you like it or not."

Morrie and Quoth slipped down the stairs behind him, blocking Heathcliff in.

"Meow!" Grimalkin leaped onto Heathcliff's shoulder, digging her claws in and shooting him an adorable look. Heathcliff sighed, but he shuffled down the stairs after me.

The perfect winter day. I crossed the landing and started down the main staircase, tugging on my woolen hat and gloves. *Maybe we could get hot chocolate from the bakery afterward. And invite Mrs. Ellis and Jonie to join us. I bet snow will wipe that scowl off her face...*

I stopped short, my breath catching in my throat.

No.

It couldn't be.

How...

The towering Christmas tree and all the presents were gone.

CHAPTER THREE

$\mathcal{M}$y whole body froze as the shock washed over me. How could the tree just be *missing?* It was here last night when I closed up the shop. I'd even left the Christmas lights on so anyone walking past on their way to the pub would see twinkling through the window and feel happy.

No way could the tree be gone. It took three people just to move it. It wasn't the sort of thing someone could just sneak out of the shop in their handbag.

But missing it was, along with all the gifts. All that remained now was a couple of broken baubles and a ring of pine needles on the rug.

No. This can't be happening.

"Ow. Why'd you put the brakes on, Sir Sourpuss?" Morrie grumbled as Heathcliff drew up sharply behind me and swore.

"Mina, what's wrong?" Quoth called from the top of the stairs.

I gulped. Cleared my throat. Found my voice. "The tree is gone."

A flurry of wings and Morrie's yelps echoed from the staircase behind me. A moment later a black raven soared down the stairwell and settled in the center of the empty rug. It paced up and down, pecking at the scattered needles. I'd never seen a bird look so despondent.

Quoth materialized again, all naked alabaster skin and sadness. He slumped on his knees, picking at the needles. "Who would do such a thing?"

"Good riddance," Heathcliff growled, settling himself into his chair. "That thing was a nuisance, and a health and safety hazard."

Quoth turned his face away. He didn't want Heathcliff to see how upset he was. I couldn't blame him. This charity was important to Quoth, not to mention the fact that half the village had already donated presents we'd somehow allowed to be stolen. Heathcliff was being callous for no good reason.

I grabbed Heathcliff's arm. "Get up."

"Why? You don't still want a snowball fight—"

"*Now.*" I dragged Heathcliff outside. The bells tinkled as we stood on the stoop. I noticed Earl Larson, one of the local homeless population who Heathcliff had befriended, sleeping under the window ledge. He stirred when he saw us, but then his tiny black kitten mewed, and he snuggled back down to keep her warm.

I glared at Heathcliff. "I know you have a bug up your arse about Christmas, but you need to cool off. This is serious. You're upsetting Quoth."

"He'll get over it." Heathcliff tried to twist out of my grasp.

"The one who needs to get over it is *you*. Leaving aside the fact that we've now got nothing to give to the charity, someone broke into the shop last night. Isn't that something you should be concerned about?"

"Shite." Heathcliff's features collapsed. For the first time ever, he looked afraid. Before I could stop him, he bolted back inside.

I followed him as he barged past Morrie and rushed over to the desk. His eyes darted frantically as he started pulling open the drawers, muttering under his breath.

"Heathcliff, what is it?"

"It's… it's here!" Heathcliff slammed the bottom drawer shut before I could look inside. He brandished a bottle of whisky.

"What's that?"

"I won it in the quiz last night. It's my Christmas treat to myself." Heathcliff uncapped the lid and held the bottle out to me. "The only way I can deal with the constant stream of jolly people traipsing through this place. At least the thieves didn't take anything of real value."

With an explosion of feathers, Quoth transformed into his raven form. He swooped into the next room, croaking corvid obscenities at the top of his lungs.

I glared at Heathcliff. "I can't believe you. You know what this tree meant to Quoth, but all you care about is your sodding alcohol. You really are behaving like a Christmas Grinch—"

The shop bell tinkled, cutting me off mid-tirade. Heathcliff's mouth set in a firm line as we stared each other down in stony silence. A moment later, DS Wilson appeared in the doorway, a tentative smile on her face and a wrapped gift in her hands. We hadn't always had the best relationship, what with her constantly being called to investigate murders at the shop. But she was nice enough, and she was also passionate about helping animals – she volunteered at the local cat sanctuary in her spare time.

"Hi, Mina, Heathcliff, James. I just came to leave a present for the charity tree. I think it's really wonderful what you're doing— hey, where's the tree?" DS Wilson glanced around the room, her eyes narrowing on Heathcliff and I. "It was here yesterday. I saw it from the street coming back from quiz night."

"Someone stole it!" I crouched down, squinting at the empty space where the tree had been, hoping to come across a clue. "Can you call Inspector Haynes? I know Jo's visiting her family, but we need a SOCO team over here to do a full sweep of the area. There's got to be some clues…"

"Ms. Wilde, you're not a detective." DS Wilson switched into cop mode. "You're not even a police officer, so please don't give me orders. Inspector Hayes is away in the Lake District for the holidays. Even if he were here, I wouldn't call him because he works homicide." DS Wilson pulled out her phone and started texting. "I'll try to pull in Inspector Drudge, not that it's even necessary. This is an open-and-shut case."

"It is?" Morrie leaned forward, his criminal mind tickled with the possibilities. "Let me guess, you have a serial tree robber working in the area? Perhaps an ex-forestry worker who lost his job when they turned that section of King's Copse wood into the Christmas tree farm…"

"It's obvious, isn't it?" DS Wilson put her hands on her hips and glared at Heathcliff. "Mr. Earnshaw has been sniping all over the village about the holiday season and the presence of the charity tree in this shop. Only yesterday, he yelled at a room full of customers and visitors that he hated the tree and Christmas."

"How do you know that?" I didn't remember DS Wilson being in the shop at the time, and I hated to see her accuse Heathcliff again.

"It was all anyone could talk about at the pub," DS Wilson glared at Heathcliff. "Which was where you were last night, drinking yourself into a rage. No one would have you on their quiz team because they were so disgusted by your remarks. Then you ran off with your prize before we'd even had the chance to take your picture in the novelty Santa hat – a town tradition that dates back to the Victorian era! Richard said you wouldn't be allowed at any more quiz nights – that's how much you've offended everyone in the village, you… you Christmas Grinch!"

Heathcliff remained bone still. He glared up at DS Wilson, his dark eyes daring her to say more. I stepped in front of him and folded my arms. "You can't just accuse Heathcliff without—"

"As an eyewitness, I'm just telling you what I saw. At one point, your boyfriend pounded his fist into a table so hard he cracked the wood. It's obvious he drank himself into a villainous mood, came here, destroyed the tree, then hid it to try and make it look like a burglary."

"What a bloody stupid theory," Heathcliff retorted. "That tree was twelve feet high. Where do you suppose I hid it? Up my arseho—"

I cut him off. "I really don't think Heathcliff is responsible. Isn't it better to approach any crime with no preconceived idea about the perpetrator?"

"That's the idea. But when all the circumstantial evidence points at one suspect…" DS Wilson tapped her phone. "Inspector Drudge has asked me to make an assessment of the scene on his behalf. I need a statement from all of you. Mina, when did you last see the tree?"

"It was here when I locked up the shop, about 6PM. I didn't come downstairs again until just now. I was in the attic with my boyfriends…" I looked around for Quoth and found him sitting on the door in his bird form. "Er, yes. I mean, in the attic with Morrie. The other flatmate, Allen, is away visiting his family."

"She's my alibi," Morrie grinned. "And I'm hers. I alibied her hard and without protection—"

"Yes, I get the idea." DS Wilson groaned. "And the two of you didn't hear anything?" She whipped her gaze from me to Morrie, struggling to keep the salacious questions out of her eyes. I never explicitly told her I was dating all the guys, but I'd never hid the truth, either. I figured in her job she'd probably seen all kinds. She desperately wanted to ask, and I admit I kind of wanted to tell her, but also, I think we both understood it was better if Argleton didn't know about my harem just yet.

"We heard the usual thuds and groans of this old building settling—oh, and I heard the bells on the door tinkle," I remembered. "I assumed it was Heathcliff coming home from the pub."

"What time was that?"

"I didn't look at a clock, but somewhere between 10:30 and 11PM?"

DS Wilson turned to Heathcliff. "Can you confirm the time you arrived home?"

Heathcliff shrugged. "Dunno. Wasn't exactly on a schedule."

I elbowed him in the ribs. *You could at least try to help yourself.* "The pub shuts at 11PM on quiz nights. Had the landlord called time?"

Heathcliff nodded. DS Wilson scribbled notes.

"And the tree was still here when you arrived home?"

"I don't know. I didn't exactly…" Heathcliff grabbed his sleeve. "Yes, it bloody well was! I was trying to get to my desk, to… to… pour another drink, and I crashed into the blasted thing and knocked it over onto the table. I was too drunk, so I figured I'd right it in the morning. Look, it shed needles all over my coat."

I had to lean in close to see the needles stuck to the fabric, but there they were, running along the inside of his arm, like he'd given the tree a hug.

I wonder if that's how the bauble ended up in the hallway upstairs, too.

DS Wilson looked unconvinced. "All that proves is you were the last person to handle the tree. Lift up your feet. Let's see the soles of your boots."

Grumbling under his breath, Heathcliff complied. DS Wilson leaned in and I stooped down to peer at his boots. Sure enough, the soles were caked with dried mud and needles.

No. I can't believe it. I refuse to believe it.

"That doesn't mean anything!" I showed her the needles stuck to my own boots. "You know those things are the herpes of the tree world. They stick to everything. They're already spread all over the shop – Heathcliff could have got them stuck all over him doing perfectly mundane daily tasks."

DS Wilson didn't acknowledge me but continued to write on

her pad. A sick feeling twisted in my stomach. Heathcliff had a *lot* more pine needles stuck to his clothing than I did.

That's because he's a filth wizard. He's probably been wearing those same clothes for days without cleaning them. And by his own admission, he crashed about in a drunken stupor last night. He probably did hug the tree. Of course he'd be covered in needles.

Someone else snuck into the shop after Heathcliff went to bed. That's the only explanation.

Next, DS Wilson inspected the floor. Now that I was looking closely, I could see needles scattered everywhere – over the nativity and books on the table, and all across the windowsill. Two more broken glass baubles lay in a forlorn heap beside Heathcliff's desk. DS Wilson collected a couple of the larger shards in an evidence bag.

"There's a horrible smell over here." She pointed to an area near the table.

I bent down and sniffed, my head spinning from the fumes. It was that gross catnip spray Mum brought in, but it was a different spot than the one Mum sprayed yesterday. DS Wilson showed me a wide circle where the rug was soaked in the stuff, and there were a few glass shards scattered at the edge.

"Mum wrapped up a bottle and placed it under the tree," I remembered. "The bottle was glass. I bet the thief broke it and left this stain."

"I agree," she said. "Perhaps the perpetrator will reek of it."

Morrie loudly sniffed Heathcliff's jacket. "It's hard to discern one scent from the layers of odor," he said. "But I do detect a hint of catnip."

"That's because Mina's mother sprayed that poxy stuff all over the shop yesterday," Heathcliff shot back.

Muddy footprints of different sizes tramped across the rugs. It would be impossible to separate the prints of our tree thief from ours or our customers. We followed the trail of needles and mud across the floor and down the hall to the front door.

Opening the door, we saw more needles on the stoop and steps before the night's snowfall obscured any possible path.

DS Wilson stooped to inspect the front door. "This lock hasn't been broken or damaged. No one forced their way in. What about other ways to get into the house?"

My stomach lurched.

I showed her the rear entrance. The lock there was also intact. We walked around the bottom story to check if any windows were broken. None were, and all the latches were shut tight.

"This building has a cellar?" DS Wilson rubbed her arms as that freezing draft whipped down the hall.

I nodded. "But it has no external window or entrance, and the vent isn't large enough for anyone to squeeze through, let alone get out with a tree. The entrance is blocked off with a bookcase. I don't even know where it is, but Morrie can show you if you want—"

But DS Wilson was already distracted by something on the staircase. I stooped down to look closely and noticed a scattering of needles trailing up the stairs. We followed the trail up to the first-floor landing, where another glass shard waited.

"What's this?" DS Wilson picked up some tufts of black fur beside the shard.

"That's the fringe on Heathcliff's coat." My stomach twisted in knots. I didn't like where this was going. "Like the needles, it's probably all over the shop…"

DS Wilson bagged the fur and held up another broken shard. "And why would this be on the stairs?"

I had no answer. My heart sinking, I followed her up the narrow stairs to our flat. The needle trail continued across the living room. In the corner beside Heathcliff's chair, DS Wilson picked up a small length of ribbon and a torn piece of gift wrap. None of us had been wrapping presents upstairs, so the only way those could have got up here was if… if…

No. It's not true.

The needles came to a stop outside the door of Heathcliff's room.

Something cold settled on my chest. I reached up to turn the knob. *I'm going to open this door and see the usual messy room and everything will be fine, because Heathcliff would never do this—*

"You're not allowed in there!" Heathcliff flung himself in front of the door, his eyes wild.

DS Wilson shot me a triumphant look. I grabbed Heathcliff's arm and tried to pry his fingers from the doorframe. "Just let her look inside. When she sees there are no presents in there, she'll know you didn't do it, and we can—"

"No." Heathcliff's dark eyes raged.

Tears pricked in the corners of my eyes. *Why didn't he want DS Wilson to see inside his bedroom? What's he hiding?*

"Why not?" I asked in a small voice.

"I'd also like to know why you don't want me to see inside this room," DS Wilson fixed Heathcliff with a suspicious stare.

"Come back with a warrant, and I'll happily let you sniff around my underthings. Until then, no one goes into this room." To emphasize his point, Heathcliff grabbed an old-fashioned key from his pocket and turned it in the lock until we all heard a loud, metallic *click*.

"Heathcliff, please—" Tears spilled over, running down my cheeks. I shook his arm, but he was as immovable as a statue. He wrenched his head away, not even looking at me.

"I think I've seen enough." DS Wilson scribbled on her pad. "There's no evidence of a break-in. The thief was either inside the house or had a key to get in. They took the tree and dragged it outside. Since you and Mr. Moriarty vouch for each other, and your other flatmate is away, it has to be Heathcliff – the one person in this room with a motive to destroy the tree."

I balled my hands into fists, fighting to gain control over my rising panic. "Heathcliff didn't do it. He'd never—"

DS Wilson flipped her pad shut and shoved it into her pocket.

"Mina, because you've helped us out with a couple of cases over the last few months, and also because Inspector Drudge hates being bothered with paperwork over the holidays, I'll tell you what I'll do. I'm going to keep this quiet for forty-eight hours. Convince your boyfriend to return the tree and presents intact, or in two days' time I'll be pressing formal charges."

CHAPTER FOUR

"I didn't do this." Heathcliff barely held himself together. His whole body trembled with rage. He planted both hands on his desk and loomed over it, looking every bit the terrifying fiend he'd been described as in *Wuthering Heights*. Needles dropped from his coat like tiny snowflakes of incrimination.

He faced off against Morrie, Quoth, and I. Between his hands was the scrap of ribbon and the broken baubles, along with the intact one I'd found in the hallway this morning. The one with tufts of his coat sticking out of it.

The only other sound in the room was Grimalkin's ecstatic mews as she rolled about in the catnip stain.

"Just admit it." Quoth's eyes blazed. "Give the tree and the presents back and we can all pretend you're not a villain."

"I can't give the bloody tree back, because I don't know where it is!"

Quoth turned his head away. "You're horrible. You don't care who you hurt, as long as you get your way."

I wrapped my arm around Quoth's shoulders, but he shrugged me off and slunk into the shadows. A moment later, a black raven swooped up to perch on the chandelier and frown down at Heathcliff.

"You going to sit up there and judge me all bloody day," Heathcliff shook his fist at the bird. "So that's what friendship means to a grim, ungainly, ghastly, gaunt and ominous bird of yore."

"Croak!" Quoth's eyes blazed with ire.

"Hey, don't get personal." I glared at Heathcliff, lest he broke into another line of Quoth's least-favorite poem. "Quoth has a right to be upset."

"Yeah. The birdie's not the only one reeling." Morrie stuck out his lower lip. "I'm hurt, too. You committed a high-stakes theft and didn't even tell me! I'm the Napoleon of Crime, in case you've forgotten. If you'd employed my help I wouldn't have allowed you to make so many stupid mistakes."

"I didn't make any stupid mistakes, because I didn't steal the bloody tree!" Heathcliff bellowed.

I struggled to keep my breathing even as I leaned over and placed my hands on top of his. Beneath my fingers, he trembled. "Heathcliff, if you tell me you didn't take the tree, then I believe you. But is there any possibility that in your inebriated state you might have done something to it? Thrown it somewhere on the street, or cut it up? Maybe if we—"

"I didn't do it. I crashed into the bloody thing when I came home, but that was it. I came upstairs and went to bed."

"Then why didn't you want DS Wilson to look in your room?"

"None of your business." He jerked his hands from under mine, making the whole desk shake.

"Fine." I closed my eyes for a moment, blinking back the tears that threatened to fall. "I stand by what I said. Even though you're being a complete wanker, I believe you. But convincing DS Wilson and the rest of the village is another matter – the four of us have to tackle this the way we settle all the other mysteries that cross our path. We've got two days to figure out who took the tree and presents and make them return it."

Morrie and Quoth looked at each other. Quoth fluttered to the ground and transformed back into his human form. Naked, he stared at the floor, his long hair curtaining his face so I couldn't see the pain in his eyes.

"I'd love to help, Mina. But I've got to head over to the animal shelter. They've got a fresh litter of rescued kittens coming in today. And now that they're not going to get all the supplies from under the tree, they need all the help..." his words faded into a shudder.

"But, Quoth—"

Quoth had already scooped up his clothes and padded away into the shadows.

I glared at Heathcliff. "You should go after him."

"Why? He's the craven one suspecting me of high crimes. He should be the one apologizing to me."

"You know he's sensitive about the animals, and yet you've been sniping at him about the tree ever since we put it up."

Heathcliff waved his arms around his head. "That's because it was bigger than the bloody shop. You know what? Go after the tree thief if you want, but leave me out of it. Thanks to this burglary I've finally got some peace and quiet, and I intend to enjoy it."

Before I could protest, Heathcliff grabbed up his prize whisky, swung around, and stumbled through to his office. *CRASH*. The door slammed behind him – the sound slicing through my fractured heart.

I stared at the cracked wood of the door. A tear escaped the corner of my eye. I couldn't believe Heathcliff would steal from the town, from me, and especially from Quoth. But between his horrible mood and the fact he wouldn't help clear his own name... was I wrong?

Did Heathcliff steal Christmas?

CHAPTER FIVE

I slid into Heathcliff's chair. The glass baubles stared up at me, mocking me with his secrets. I shoved them aside and pulled over a notebook and pen.

Time to get to work. Detective Mina is in.

"Does anyone else have a key to the shop?" I asked Morrie, who was busy picking needles off his favorite velvet chair.

Morrie sat down. He winced. Reaching under his arse, he pulled out a particularly long needle and tossed it aside in disgust. "So you *are* trying to solve the theft."

"Of course I am."

"Even though it might reveal Heathcliff was the thieving bastard who took all those donated gifts?"

"It's not going to reveal that, because Heathcliff wouldn't do such a horrible thing," I said with more conviction than I felt. I truly believed Heathcliff was innocent, but so much evidence had mounted against him and he was refusing to help himself.

He was acting guilty. I *hated* it.

Morrie brushed needles off the edge of the desk and leaned across to fix me with his icicle eyes. "You know I can't refuse a good mystery. What do you have so far?"

I doodled names on the page. "It wasn't Heathcliff, and it wasn't Quoth or you or I. Grimalkin lacks opposable thumbs, so it can't possibly be her. It had to have been someone outside the shop. I've checked the bedroom upstairs and it's locked tight, so it wasn't someone who's come from some other place in time. We haven't seen any new fictional characters around. Judging by the fact the thieves absconded the tree out the front door, I think we're looking at ordinary, human crooks from this century, probably one that now smells like catnip. Since the burglar didn't break any locks or windows, they must have a key. Do you know if Heathcliff has given anyone a copy of the key?"

"Are you kidding? He won't even give Quoth and I keys. I wouldn't have stood for it except that he doesn't know I can pick the lock in about two seconds flat. You're the only one who has one. Oh, and Bertie the accountant."

"He does?" That seemed weird.

"Sure. One day a few years back, Bertie needed to collect the account ledger, but Heathcliff was passed out drunk. Rather than have his client face a late payment fee, Bertie broke a window, climbed inside, collected the ledger, and left a note stuck to Heathcliff's forehead saying he either needed to move to cloud-based accounting software or give Bertie a key to the shop."

I couldn't resist a smile at that. "Heathcliff would never agree to voluntarily use the computer."

"Exactly. Hence, Bertie got his key. Just as well, too – he cut up his abdomen pretty bad on the broken window. There was blood *everywhere*. I think he's been a bit afraid of Heathcliff ever since – he keeps hinting that Heathcliff finds another accountant, but you know how much that guy likes change. Heathcliff is by far Bertie's most bothersome client, so maybe he thought if he could frame Heathcliff for the robbery he'd be able to get out of their contract, but that seems a pretty feeble reason to steal the tree."

"Except that Bertie's dog just had puppies!" I exclaimed. "He said his wife lost her job and he was struggling to feed them. If you were desperate, and you knew where some pet supplies were, and you had a key and a guy you didn't like took the fall for it, that sounds like an ideal solution to me."

"Clever girl." Morrie grinned. Figuring out motive was his favorite part of solving crimes. He loved delving into the seedy and easily corruptible minds of humans.

I underlined Bertie's name three times. On the rug in front of me, Grimalkin darted and danced between the two catnip-soaked spots. Even though Quoth had scrubbed the stains with industrial cleaner and the place no longer smelled like a sewage-treatment plant, Grimalkin's sensitive nose was still attracted to the lingering residue. She'd roll around on the carpet for a few minutes, then shoot up one of the bookcases, knock down an avalanche of hardcovers on our heads, tumble off the end, land on her feet and start the whole cycle again.

"Anyone else with a key?" I asked, dodging a falling Dickens as Grimalkin tore along the Classics shelf.

Morrie shrugged. "Not that I can think of. Didn't you give a key to that lady making the calendar?"

"That's right!" I scribbled Tabitha's name. "We'll have to find out where she was last night, see if she has an alibi. She also heard Heathcliff bitching about the tree, so she knew he'd be the perfect person to pin the robbery on. But what I don't get is her motive—what are you doing? You're disturbing our crime scene!"

Morrie had risen from the chair and was scrambling around under the windowsill on his hands and knees. He held up something between his fingers that glittered in the light. "What I'm doing is finding the clue that will blow this case wide open. Will you look at this?"

"Bring it over here. I can't see."

Morrie dropped the object on the desk in front of me. I held it up to inspect it. An earring – an enormous chunk of polished black crystal wound with wire and fixed to a silver butterfly. It looked handmade. And familiar, but I couldn't think of where I'd seen it before.

"It's not mine, and I don't think this was left behind by a customer. No one would have been able to get around that side of the tree without some serious acrobatics. This was dropped by our tree thief!"

"Which means it probably wasn't Bertie," Morrie pointed out. "He doesn't look like an earring sort of guy."

"Maybe not, but we can't rule him out yet." I slipped the earring into my pocket. It was the first serious clue we had so far. "I'll ask around about it at the market tonight. The village gossip train will be hard at work. I bet we'll be able to find the owner of this earring and clear Heathcliff's name."

CHAPTER SIX

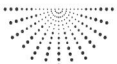

*A*ll day, villagers arrived in the shop bearing armloads of gifts for the charity tree. Over and over again I had to tell the story of how the tree had been stolen overnight. Faces pinched. Mothers and children exchanged knowing looks. The accusation hung in the air, unspoken but heard loud and clear – *Heathcliff stole the tree. Heathcliff hates Christmas. Heathcliff hates the village.*

"You can leave your gifts with me," I begged David Hyde and his son. "We're organizing a replacement tree. I'll make sure everything is locked away and makes it to the animal shelter."

"Sorry, Mina." David – a regular customer and British canal history buff who loved to haggle over the price of books so fervently Heathcliff now priced every canal history book £2 more than he expected to profit from it in expectation of David's protests – shoved his son toward the door. "I think we'll just deliver these to the shelter ourselves this year."

Despite the beautiful displays I'd put together and the Christmas book specials we'd advertised in the local paper, we had hardly any sales. I heard people muttering as they left the shop, watched them whisper together out on the street, pointing to Nevermore's windows with judgmental frowns. Heathcliff didn't emerge from his study all day. I didn't know if that was for the best or not. The village had turned on him again. It was vital we put in an upbeat appearance at the market and didn't do anything to further cast suspicion on Heathcliff.

I thought I'd have a battle to get Heathcliff out the door, but just as I was shutting up the shop, he emerged, looking every bit as sullen and bitter as he had that morning. "I'm showering." He slipped past me without meeting my gaze and trudged up the stairs.

The three of us gathered in the front hall to wait for him. I was pleased Heathcliff was making an effort to dress up, since everyone else had. For Morrie that meant an exquisitely-tailored black suit with a black wool coat. I donned a crimson bodycon sweater dress I'd studded with glittering rhinestones over black leggings and knee-high laced boots. Quoth remained in his raven form – apparently, feathers were more insulating against the winter chill than anything else in his closet. He'd freshly preened and had even donned a tiny Santa hat for the occasion.

"Are you sure it's a good idea for Lord Sourpuss to go tonight?" Morrie whispered.

"I think his absence will be noted," I whispered back. "Besides, maybe the twinkling lights and music and food will knock him out of his Christmas funk and he'll—"

"He'll what? Apologize to Quoth? Suddenly express goodwill to all mankind? Be visited by three obnoxious ghosts that help him realize the true meaning of Christmas? That's what I love about you, gorgeous. Your undying belief in the goodness in people, despite all evidence to the contrary. Heathcliff—"

"What about Heathcliff?"

I glanced up. At first, all I saw was shadow, but then my brooding anti-hero descended the stairs like he was attending his own funeral. He'd donned a pair of black cargo pants that at least had no noticeable holes, a white shirt, red vest, and his black wool coat with the frayed fur trim. With his filthy boots, wild eyes, and unkempt hair (the way it was *still* unkempt after just showering was one of the many mysteries of Heathcliff) he looked every bit like the hellion who'd just stepped off the moors.

"Let's just get this ordeal over with," Heathcliff muttered as he helped me wind my scarf around my neck.

"You might not be excited, but I can't wait." Every year since I could remember, I'd attended the Argleton Christmas market. Usually, I went with my best friend Ashley and her family, because Mum would be behind a stall trying to hawk smoothie packs or ugly leggings or whichever wacky pyramid scheme she was involved in at the time. I felt a faint twinge of sadness that Ashley wouldn't be there this year – she'd been murdered only a few months ago. Even though we were no longer friends at the time, I still felt her loss like a punch in the gut.

But it was quickly replaced by a sizzle of excitement. For the first time ever, I'd be going with my *boyfriends.* I linked arms with Heathcliff and Morrie. Quoth hopped onto my shoulder as we walked out the door of Nevermore Bookshop and were transported to a new world.

Mrs. Ellis and her committee transformed the town green into a Christmas wonderland, with strings of colored fairy lights looped between the lamp posts and bedecking the statue of the town's founder. Delicious Christmassy smells wafted from a line of food trucks parked opposite the pub, which had a license to serve drinks on the green for tonight only. I breathed in deep the mingled scents of mulled wine, fruit mince pies, hot roasted nuts, roast beef smothered with gravy, and Yorkshire puddings as big as my head.

Stalls around the perimeter sold Christmas goodies – wooden toys, baby clothes, knitted beanies and scarves covered with rows of jaunty reindeer, dollhouse furniture, teddy bears of all shapes and colors, homemade fudge and artisan cheeses. I waved to Mum, who was busy showing off her fancy wrapping papers to a gaggle of excited women. In the stall next to her, my eyes picked up the twinkle of jewelry. As my eyesight got worse, I discovered I derived a kind of visual joy from seeing sparkles and twinkles. I dragged the boys over to the jewelry stand.

"Look at these!" I held up a pendant containing an amethyst set into three bird claws. "This is really cool."

"I make all these myself," a familiar voice said. I turned to see Elizabeth, Bertie's wife, grinning at me from behind the counter.

"Wow, I had no idea. You're so talented." I swung the necklace rack in a slow circle, leaning close to make out the details of the intricate pendants.

"Thank you. Can I help you pick out something?" She winked at the guys. "Perhaps whichever one of these lads is your boyfriend might like to buy you an early Christmas present?"

Please, not more presents.

But it was too late, Heathcliff had already pulled out his wallet. Grinning, Elizabeth held a necklace up beside my face.

"I think this brings out the color of your eyes." She handed me a mirror and unclasped the necklace. "And I've got matching earrings, but they're not on display. I'll show you after I've secured this…"

"Let me." Heathcliff took the necklace from her hands and draped the chain around my neck. I squinted at the mirror while Elizabeth hunted around in the back of her stall. Morrie spun an earring rack. As colors and stones whirled past, something caught my eye.

"Wait." I stopped the earring rank mid-spin. "Look at these."

I held a pair of enormous black stone earrings up to Morrie. He shook his head. "Those are totally wrong for your coloring. They're perfect for Heathcliff, though. They'd bring out the rage in his eyes."

I shoved them closer to Morrie's face. "Look closer. They're the same as the earring we found in the shop."

"Croak?" Quoth tapped the earrings with his beak.

Elizabeth stared at us, her smile frozen, not sure how to react. "Did you want those hematite earrings, Mina?"

"No thanks. I noticed them because we found an earring on the floor of the shop that's identical to these. They're so beautiful, I'd love to be able to return it to its owner." I flashed a sweet smile as I pulled the earring out of my pocket. "Can you help us find the owner? If you keep a record of who buys from you—"

Elizabeth shook her head. "I'm afraid I'm not as sophisticated as all that. Although I'm sure Bertie will get his way eventually and I'll have my whole business online. He's always going on about the power of cloud computing for small business—"

"I think Bertie's going to bring this whole village kicking and screaming into the 21st century," I laughed. "But back to these earrings. Do you sell many of this particular design?"

"Not really. They's a little large and dark for most people. Most ladies prefer the daintier styles they can wear every day."

As Elizabeth turned, I noticed a few sparkly beads sticking out of the back of her sweater. "It looks like you're using yourself as a display stand." I pointed to the rogue craft supplies.

"Oh, silly me. I must've leaned back over my craft table again." Elizabeth laughed, pulling off the beads. "It's these winter woollies – everything sticks to them, especially jewelry. Why, often my husband will leave the house with one of my earrings stuck to his suit and he won't even notice!"

A thought occurred to me. "You haven't noticed any of your own supplies of these earrings gone missing?"

"Why, yes, actually." Elizabeth frowned. "It was those black earrings you're holding. I had two pairs on my craft table, and this morning when I packed up for the market one earring was missing. I bet Bertie snagged it on his sweater and dropped it when he visited last night. I always tell him to check himself before he goes outside, but he never listens. If it's not numbers or spreadsheets, he's completely hopeless."

"Bertie came over to the shop… last night?" Morrie leaned forward, his eyes twinkling with the scent of an important clue.

"Yes. It was probably around 11:30PM. He left an important piece of paper in Heathcliff's office, and he wanted it so he could finish the accounts last night. I said you'd all be asleep and he needed to wait for morning, but he swore he'd just pop in and out, all quiet-like." She lowered her voice. "Between you and me, he's been under a lot of stress lately, what with me losing my job and Princess' new puppies. He was going to give you the accounts today so he could get paid and we'd have a bit of money over Christmas, but then we heard about the terrible robbery, and he didn't want to bother you all."

I bet he didn't. If Bertie had accidentally snagged the earring on his coat, and he'd been in the shop last night after Heathcliff got home, he could be the Christmas thief.

"It's just horrible," Elizabeth continued. "I can't imagine who would commit such a heinous crime. It must've been someone who truly hates Christmas…"

Her voice trailed off as Heathcliff's eyes bore into her. She straightened up. He'd come to the same conclusion as I had about Bertie, but Elizabeth had also just realized who would be the likely suspect, and she mistook Heathcliff's suspicion for guilt. She straightened up and her voice took on a businesslike tone. "Well, anyway, I hope they catch the bastard who did it. I'll wrap up the necklace for you and you can be on your way."

While Heathcliff paid for my necklace, Morrie and I exchanged a look. We needed to find Bertie and wrestle the truth from him somehow.

As I accepted my wrapped necklace, Tabitha bustled over. "Hi, Mina. Hi, boys. Elizabeth, I'm so pleased to see you. I wondered if you might be able to help me. I've lost one of your lovely hematite earrings."

"You have?" Elizabeth turned to me. "Mina, isn't this fortu-itous? I remember now that Tabitha purchased a set of those exact earrings from me six months ago. So maybe the one you found in the bookshop wasn't mine after all."

Tabitha lost an earring? Interesting.

"You found an earring in the bookshop?" Tabitha backed away, her eyes darting from me to Heathcliff. "Er... it can't possibly be mine. I lost my earring a week ago, so I definitely wasn't wearing them yesterday when I visited the shop. I've got to go – I need to get my beauty sleep if I'm to be up bright and early for the shoot tomorrow."

Oh, she must not have heard. "Actually, Tabitha, the tree was—"

But Tabitha cut me off before I could finish. She backed away, her eyes darting toward the pub. "Elizabeth, I can see you're busy, so I... I'll talk to you later."

Watching Tabitha dash across the green, a nagging feeling prickled behind my eyes. I remembered why those earrings looked familiar to me. Tabitha *had* been wearing them when she came to talk to me in the shop yesterday. Normally, I'd be too blind to notice, but those stones were so big they stuck out.

Which meant Tabitha was lying. And she was acting very cagey. But why?

Bertie or Tabitha? We still had two potential suspects. But how to figure out which one of them had taken the gifts?

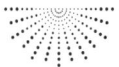

CHAPTER SEVEN

"It's got to be the accountant." Morrie frowned at the wine swirling in the bottom of his glass. "I never did trust him. He always looked far too happy about spreadsheets."

"Of course you don't trust him. You run a criminal empire out of Nevermore Bookshop and you don't want to get caught. I'm not sure your opinion counts for much in this case."

Morrie pushed his glass away in disgust. I didn't know why he kept ordering wine from the Rose & Wimple – it never lived up to his exacting standards. "On the contrary. It takes one to know one, and Bernie Robinson has the cold, dead eyes of a villainous Christmas thief."

"Croak!" Quoth nodded his head vigorously as he plunged his beak into the peanut bowl.

The four of us crowded around a table at the pub, sipping drinks (mine was a hot toddy, of course) and listening to Mrs. Ellis warble along to "I Saw Mommy Kissing Santa Claus" on the village karaoke machine. Hardly anyone spoke to us, and villagers shot daggers at Heathcliff across the room. Word about the robbery had already spread, and Argleton wasted no time in acting as judge and jury.

"Speaking of Bertie," Morrie gestured out the window. "He's walking his motive around the green."

I had to cup my hands on the window in order to see. I could just make out a figure being dragged along by a large golden retriever and five adorable puppies. Excited barks and yips penetrated Mrs. Ellis' song. *Bertie had the means and the motive, but I can't imagine him stealing from a charity.*

"It just doesn't seem like him." I watched Bernie stop to chat with Mrs. Ellis' granddaughter Jonie. Jonie's face lit up as she bent to pet the puppies, transforming her from a sullen pre-teen into a pretty, happy animal lover. Bertie lifted one of the dogs into her waiting arms, and Jonie laughed as it licked her cheek. "I can't see him stealing presents meant for a charity. And if he did take the presents, why take the tree as well? Do we really think Bertie dragged that heavy thing outside all by himself? I'm more interested in Tabitha and her missing earring."

"She has no motive. Right now we don't even have proof she was in the shop that evening. And she doesn't smell like catnip."

"Neither does Bertie. Besides, we do have proof." I dropped the earring on the table. Quoth picked it up and dangled it from his beak. "She lied about losing her earring a week ago. I saw her wearing these when she came in to speak to me about the calendar. She didn't leave it then because you found it near the back of the tree. No one could have got around the tree unless they were the ones carting it off."

"But the earring could also have been attached to Bertie's jacket," Morrie said. "We know from Curmudgeonly Cathy Lover over here how easily things can stick to clothes."

I glanced over at Heathcliff, remembering all those pine needles stuck to his clothes. *Of course, he'd have that many needles stuck to him if he staggered into the tree. It doesn't mean he carried it outside.*

It *doesn't.*

"Don't use that name," Heathcliff growled. He referred, of

course, to Cathy – his great love from *Wuthering Heights*. The woman who had rejected him shortly before he found his way into the real world and my arms. His ex. Even though she didn't exist in our world, I'd found Cathy a little threatening in the beginning – Heathcliff and Cathy *were* literature's greatest lovers – but now I was confident enough in myself to know that when Heathcliff said he was over her, he meant it.

Morrie swiped Heathcliff's hot toddy and took a long sip. "That still doesn't solve the issue of motive. Tabitha has no reason to want to steal the Christmas tree."

"No reason that we know of." I watched as Tabitha entered the room, her arm looped in a tall, dark, and handsome stranger. I pushed my chair back. "But I bet she has one. I'm going to find out."

"Croak." Quoth settled on my shoulder, his talons digging into my sweater dress. *I'm coming with you.*

I made my way across the room to the bar. The stranger leaned in close to whisper something in Tabitha's ear. She threw her head back and gave a tinkling laugh, tossing her hair over her shoulder in what I could only describe as a classic Ashley flirting move.

"Tabitha, hi!" I slid into the empty seat beside her, leaning back as her vanilla perfume smacked me in the face. *Is she drowning herself in perfume to disguise the smell of catnip?* "I just wanted to say how excited we are to have you shoot the calendar at Nevermore—"

The words dried in my throat as I recognized the guy she was with. Sitting on a sticky barstool in the Rose & Wimple pub was none other than the world-famous photographer Roland Crabapple.

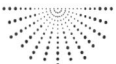

ina, you've gone all stiff. Quoth's voice pounded inside my skull. *What's wrong?*

"H-h-h-hi," I stammered, completely taken aback.

I'd met famous fashion people before. Hell, I used to intern for the avant-garde New York Designer Marcus Ribald. But there were famous fashion people, and then there was *Roland fucking Crabapple.* When Tabitha said she'd booked him to shoot the calendar, I'd half-assumed she'd been scammed, and some white-headed grandpa who spent his weekends taking pictures of steam locomotives would show up.

"Mina, have you met Roland?" Tabitha leaned back on her stool and touched the photographer's arm with a kind of posses-sive claw. Her attitude was as brazen as her outfit – a bright red figure-hugging dress, giant dangling earrings sparkling with diamonds, and a long fur coat. She didn't have any qualms about showing off Roland around the village, even though half of them had grown up with her husband.

"Hello." Roland reached out to shake my hand. His skin felt cold and clammy. Even though I couldn't see him doing it, I *felt* his eyes raking over my body. Fashion photographers were often kind of sleazy, but Roland made my skin crawl. "You have quite the sense of style, Mina. I didn't expect to meet such chic ladies on my trip to the middle of nowhere."

"Mina used to work in the fashion industry," Tabitha cooed. "She's way too glamorous for us Argleton-bunnies."

"I-I-I thought you weren't coming in until tomorrow morning," I stammered out.

"I've actually been in the village for a couple of days." Roland snapped his fingers to signal the landlord like he was some fancy Lord ordering around a butler. When Richard came over to serve us, he looked annoyed. He slammed glasses of mulled wine in front of Roland and Tabitha and turned away without a word. "I'm intrigued by your little charity venture. It combined two of my favorite things – Christmas trees and caring for animals. I have a cat of my own, so I know how important it is that they be cared for to a high standard. I'd have stopped by to introduce myself and take a look at the space, but Tabitha has kept me busy."

"Roland has been... tied up with appointments," Tabitha explained in a simpering voice.

"I think you mean, I've tied you up," Roland purred, leaning in to place a wet kiss on Tabitha's cheek. His hand wrapped possessively around her waist. It was then that I noticed the black choker around Tabitha's neck had a tiny gold chain attached, which extended to a ring Roland wore on his finger.

Ew. Gross.

I mean, I was all for a little experimentation. Morrie had handcuffs and all sorts of fun things in his room. But Roland Crabapple was old and gross. I'd never want his cold hands anywhere near me.

"Mmmm," Tabitha purred, leaning back against Roland and tilting her chin back, exposing her neck for another of his wet kisses. "It has been quite a… pleasurable trip. I've been showing Roland the sights of Argleton. We spent all day yesterday visiting the arboretum and the botanical gardens. Roland gets so excited around plants and trees, it's positively enthralling…"

"Yes, the wonders of nature inspire my work. If you'll excuse me, ladies. I need the gents." Roland flashed me a sleazy smile before reaching up to unbuckle the chain from Tabitha's neck so he could slide into the crowd.

Tabitha leaned over, a devilish smile on her face. "He's amazing. Isn't he?"

"Um, sure. He's shot some iconic designers. Are you sure he's the right fit for the Argleton charity calendar?"

"Of course," Tabitha beamed. "Only the best for our village. Now, you haven't forgotten we'll be there bright and early at 5AM. Is it okay if I move around the decorations on the tree? Roland will need things to be just so—"

"That's just the thing, Tabitha. There's no tree. Someone stole it last night."

She gasped. "That's horrible."

Her surprise seemed to be genuine, but she could just be a good actress.

"Yes, it is. All the presents for the charity are gone, too." I slipped the earring out of my purse. I had a better plan for how I'd catch our thief. "Luckily, I know people who can help us get to the bottom of the mystery. We'll bring down the full force of the law on their asses. My flatmate Jo happens to be a forensics expert. She's coming in first thing tomorrow to do a full investigation. The police are, of course, taking this matter very seriously. I'm confident that anyone sneaking around in our shop will be in for a nasty surprise when DS Wilson comes knocking."

"Oh, no," Tabitha breathed.

"Oh, yes." I nodded vigorously. "The robber dropped this earring. Tonight when we get back to the shop, I'm going to place it into an evidence bag and leave it on Heathcliff's desk for Jo to analyze. I'm sure she'll find traces of DNA that can link us to the thief."

"That's a good idea," Tabitha said weakly, knocking back her wine in a single gulp and reaching for Roland's. "This villain must pay."

"I couldn't agree more." I slipped the earring back into my pocket.

Roland returned from the bathroom. "I wanted to ask you, Mina. Would we be able to borrow your bird for our photo shoot? He's quite a remarkable creature."

"Croak," Quoth agreed with Roland's assessment. *If only he knew.*

"I've been telling Roland all about the raven," Tabitha said, finishing off Roland's wine. "How Quoth is kind of a store mascot, and how that Mr. Heathcliff seems like a grumpy old brute but actually saves all these animals. First that bird, and then that grumpy cat. He doesn't even mind all the defecation."

"I feel a personal affinity to ravens," Roland reached over to pet Quoth's head. "They're some of the most intelligent animals to exist. And this guy reminds me of that poem, 'Once upon a midnight dreary. While I pondered, weak and weary—'"

"Croak." Quoth shot the photographer a warning look.

"I wouldn't do that if I were you," I said.

But Roland was on a roll. "I studied the classics at Cambridge, you see. I'm a lover of great literature. I can recite the great works by heart. 'Over many a quaint and curious volume of forgotten lore—'"

"Croak." Quoth flapped his wings and took off, hovering just above Roland's head. *This is your last warning.*

"While I nodded, nearly napping, suddenly there came a tapping, As of someone gently rapping, rapping at my chamber door—"

"Croak!"

SPLAT.

I whipped out my phone and snapped a picture just a giant glob of raven poop landed on Roland Crabapple's bald head.

"Thanks, Roland," I said brightly. "That one's for the shop's Christmas cards."

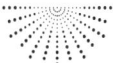

CHAPTER NINE

"*D*o you want me to wait up with you?" Heathcliff asked as I smoothed a blanket over the leather couch. We'd spent the rest of the evening *not-so-subtly* spreading the word around the fete that Jo would be conducting her forensic investigation. If a guilty party wanted to wipe any remaining prints or evidence from the scene, or recover their lost earring from Heathcliff's desk, they'd have to sneak back into the shop tonight. I'd be here waiting for them.

Jo was visiting her cousins in Scotland for the holidays. Even if she were home, she probably wouldn't conduct a full-on forensic investigation for a Christmas tree robbery, but the village didn't need to know that.

"Croak!" Quoth protested, hopping across my pillow. *I'm watching out for you, and I don't want him here.*

I shook my head at Heathcliff. "That's okay. I've got Quoth. You go to bed."

Heathcliff's eyes bore into mine. I'd hurt him by refusing his help. I wondered if the offer was his way of reaching out. Maybe he was trying to get me alone so he could talk to me about what was bothering him. I opened my mouth to say I'd changed my mind, but Heathcliff was already stomping up the stairs.

I sighed and turned back to the couch. A beautiful, naked boy sat where the raven had been only moments before. "Good riddance," Quoth growled, flipping his silken hair over his shoulder.

"Don't be like that. I think he wanted to talk to me," I said. "Maybe if we both went to him together and—"

"I don't want to talk to Heathcliff. Or about Heathcliff." Quoth reached up and pulled the cord to turn off the light. Except for a string of fairy lights looped over the balustrade, Nevermore Bookshop was plunged into darkness. The mysterious draft whipped through the room, kissing my skin with ice. Quoth shuddered and pulled me closer.

Shrouded by darkness, Quoth and I whispered together. Mostly, I let him talk, expressing his frustration and suspicion of Heathcliff in a wave of bitter resentment that sounded nothing like the Quoth I knew. I held him tight and wished I could reassure him that we'd find who really did this and get the presents back and he and Heathcliff could go back to being friends, but I wasn't sure I was as convincing as I hoped.

The only way to repair their friendship now was to prove Heathcliff didn't steal the tree. Quoth realized that too. It was why he was here with me, waiting in the gloom for something to happen—

A key turned in the lock. My breath hitched. I stiffened, freezing in place lest a movement should give away our vigil. In my arms, Quoth's body shifted, silently retracting into itself as feathers poked through his skin. A moment later, a bird of shadow scrambled out of my arms and went to wait in ambush.

Creak. The door swung inward.

Creak. Creeeeeak.

Someone tiptoed across the hallway. A shadow blocked the fairy lights as the intruder hovered in the doorway, fumbling for a flashlight. Quoth dived from the bust, croaking at full volume as he flapped his wings in the intruder's face.

"Argh, help, help!" the intruder cried.

"Ah, hah!" I cried in triumph, leaping up from the desk and flicking on the light. Tabitha's face glowed with terror as she flapped her hands uselessly at Quoth, who flew at her with the full fury of a bird slighted.

CHAPTER TEN

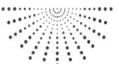

"What are you doing here, Tabitha?" I demanded.

"I'm… I'm…" She ducked as Quoth grabbed the collar of her coat and tried to tug it over her head. "Get this bird off me! He probably has rabies."

"Croak!" Quoth butted her with his head. *I resent that.*

"You're perfectly safe. He doesn't have rabies, and I promise he won't attack you anymore." I held up my arm and Quoth fluttered over to rest. "Provided that you answer my question. You can't be setting up for the photo shoot, because I already told you it's postponed. So why did you break into the shop?"

Tabitha's lip trembled. "Technically, I didn't break in. You gave me a key."

"Croak!" Quoth glared at her with those yellow eyes. Tabitha whimpered. She collapsed into the velvet chair, her shoulders sagging.

"Fine. I came to try and find my missing earring. Because… because Roland and I came here last night to shag under the tree, and I lost it."

Of all the things I expected her to say, that was not one of them. "You… what?"

"It's one of Roland's little traditions. You know artists – sex and inspiration are entwined. Before a shoot, Roland likes to make love to one of the models on set. It's part of his creative process. And when he heard the set was an enormous Christmas tree, he was even more excited. He believes sex in nature imbues the air with a kind of activated magic—"

"Let me get this straight, you and Roland Crabapple were downstairs last night, shagging under the tree?"

"Well, we *tried* to do it under the tree. It had tipped over onto the table, so there was some space back here." She pointed. "But there were so many presents, it was a bit awkward. And then Roland's foot bumped the stand and the tree toppled over onto the floor." She shrugged sheepishly. "So instead, he bent me over the desk."

I leaped up from the desk, yanking my hands back. *I'm going to need a powerful disinfectant. No, no, Roland Crabapple might have touched it with his... I think it's a goner. We need to burn the desk and salt the earth around it.*

"What time was this?"

"We got here just after midnight. I know because Roland wanted to wait until the church clock struck twelve. That's another part of his tradition."

My heart leaped with joy. If the tree was still here when Roland and Tabitha were doing their thing at midnight, that meant Heathcliff hadn't gotten rid of it when he arrived home for the pub. This proves that Heathcliff didn't—

No, it proved nothing. DS Wilson would still argue that Heathcliff could have come back down and got rid of the tree after Roland and Tabitha left. Besides, I already knew Heathcliff didn't do it, but that hadn't gotten us any closer to restoring the tree and gifts.

If she hadn't taken the tree, Tabitha had been the last person to see it intact. Or at least, semi-intact. I swiped my hand through the pile of needles on the table. *Now we know why there are so many needles here.* "Apart from knocking over the tree, you didn't touch any of the presents? Roland couldn't have taken them—"

"Oh, no, we left with everything we came with, and nothing else." Tabitha gave me a sheepish smile. "Except for my earring. I knew if your forensics friend found it, I'd get pulled in for questioning and I'd have to admit what Roland and I were doing. Oh, and as I was gathering up my clothes, I stood on a present and broke it – I ended up covered in this foul-smelling liquid."

The catnip.

"Roland was outside waiting for me, so luckily he didn't get any on him. It took me hours in the shower to get the smell out!" Tabitha continued. "No wonder Roland ran away."

Wait, what? I leaned forward. "Where did Roland go?"

"I don't know! We had a room together at the Argleton Arms, but he never came back. He sent me a text in the morning and I met him for breakfast. His clothes were all rumpled and filthy. He said he'd gone for a walk in King's Copse, and was video-chatting with his cat and lost track of time. But what does that even mean?"

"No idea." If Roland was MIA during the night, did that mean he could have come back to the shop to steal the tree and presents? "Did you know if you still had my key when you got back to the hotel?"

"I didn't look. I was so anxious to get the smell off me. But it was in my coat pocket after breakfast." Tabitha wrapped my hand in hers, her eyes pleading with me. "Mina – please keep my secret? Roland and I didn't take the presents, and I can't have a criminal record. I wouldn't be able to do my charity work. And then my husband would find out and the gossip would ruin us."

Then maybe you shouldn't have slept with a sleazy photographer in someone else's shop, I felt like saying, but that wasn't fair. I didn't know Tabitha's situation and I wasn't going to slut-shame her for her bad decisions. "I'm only interested in returning the tree and presents. Everyone thinks Heathcliff did it."

"Well, he *was* very negative," Tabitha sniffed. "I don't understand how it's possible to hate Christmas so much. Yes, carols are annoying, but there was no call for such rudeness toward those of us trying to do good in the community."

I couldn't argue with that. "Is it possible someone snuck inside while you were... um... occupied?"

"I guess so? We left the door unlocked while we got down and dirty. Roland had a whole bag full of toys." Tabitha tugged the collar around her throat. "He does things with a feather that would make your bird friend blush."

"Croak?" Quoth looked horrified. I might've burst out laughing if I wasn't so busy trying to rub away any Roland residue from my hands. "You didn't see anyone else near the shop when you entered or left?"

"I don't think so... oh, yes, actually. That vagrant fellow. Earl? He was sitting under the window ledge when we left. We even had a little chat."

"With Earl?" The homeless man was not known to be especially chatty. One of the few people he got along with was Heathcliff, and that was because neither of them uttered more than two syllables to the other if they could help it.

"Yes," Tabitha giggled. "It was so funny. Earl asked me why the tree was gone from the window, and I said Mr. Heathcliff had thrown it down in a fit of rage and declared he didn't want it! Earl had no idea what we were up to. Let me tell you, woman to woman, the thrill of getting caught makes it even more exciting—"

"Yes, well, I'm sure." I held out my hand. "Just to be safe, I'll have my key back."

Tabitha fished it from her pocket and dropped it into my hand. "I guess I'll be off now. Thank you for your discretion. If I hear anything on the village grapevine about the tree, I'll make sure to pass it on."

"I appreciate it, Tabitha." She ducked outside.

As soon as the door blew shut, Quoth fluttered down and shifted to his human form. "We have our answer. Tabitha wasn't the thief. Will you come up to bed now? It's freezing down here."

My teeth chattered as the draft blasted through the room. "Not quite yet." I pinched the corner off my favorite notebook, lifting it gingerly off the desk and dropping it into the bin. "I need to disinfect this desk first."

As I scrubbed at the wood with the industrial cleaner, my mind whirled with what we'd learned. So Earl had been outside that night, *and* he was asking about the tree. I'd better have a talk with him tomorrow.

CHAPTER ELEVEN

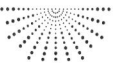

I woke up with a start – driven from dreams not by the light streaming in the attic window but by a cold blast attacking my face. That damn draft again – it was everywhere in the shop. I climbed out of bed, pulled on my fleece leggings, wool jumper, Quoth's Blood Lust hoodie, my winter trench coat, and a pair of red gloves. I wrapped my favorite red scarf several times around my neck. Still, I felt cold.

"We've really got to fix that draft," I muttered as I slunk into the kitchen, hunting on the counter for hair clips I'd left there last night. They were nowhere to be seen. Morrie was standing over the stove, layered up with a similar array of jumpers and jackets, as he hopped from foot to foot with impatience waiting for the kettle to boil.

"I would fix it if I could locate the source." The kettle whistled. Morrie poured water into two waiting cups and handed me my first tea of the day. For a few moments, we sipped in companionable silence, letting the warmth of the mugs permeate our freezing hands.

When my mouth had warmed up enough to speak, I told

Morrie what I'd learned. His lips twitched into a smirk as I told him what Tabitha and Roland had been up to.

"So everyone was getting some that night except Heathcliff. No wonder he was pissed at that tree."

Quoth fluttered downstairs and perched on my shoulder. I held out my cup to him and he dipped his head in to finish off my tea. "Quoth and I are going out to speak with Earl. Do you want to come?"

"No can do. I'm going to spend the day tailing Bertie Robinson. I hope I catch him in sordid and depraved acts. Take Heathcliff with you – he might be able to get a coherent answer out of his friend Earl."

Quoth shook his head so vigorously he nearly knocked the cup from my hands.

"I think we'll try on our own first," I said hurriedly, just as Heathcliff emerged from his room and loped into the kitchen.

"Coffee," he muttered, reaching for the kettle. He dumped three teaspoons of instant coffee into his cup, then pulled a hip flask from his pocket and added a generous glug. Even Morrie raised an eyebrow.

Quoth launched himself off my shoulder and swooped from the room. Heathcliff didn't look up. I hated that they were fighting.

"We need to talk." I grabbed Heathcliff's arm and dragged him into the living room. He slumped down in his chair and took a swig of coffee. "What is up with you?"

"I'm being falsely accused of a crime," Heathcliff muttered into his drink.

"And we're all trying to help with that. But you've been in a bad way ever since the calendar rolled over to December 1st. It's not just Christmas carols and happy customers getting you down."

"I'm a cantankerous hellion. That's my nature," he shot back.

"True. But this is different. You're acting cagey – not wanting me to go in your room. Slamming the drawer of your desk shut before I could look inside. Shutting down when I try to ask you what's wrong."

"That's because *nothing's* wrong, except that you keep harassing me." Heathcliff fixed his gaze on the corner of the room and sipped his coffee. The only clue that he still acknowledged my presence was the tension tugging at his shoulders.

"Fine." I balled my hands into fists. I willed him to look at me, to meet my eyes and see that he was hurting me, to give a shit about the people who cared for him. But he didn't look up from his drink.

Screw this. I spun on my heel and stomped down the stairs. Quoth fluttered down after me, settling on my shoulder as I dragged out the phone book to search for the number of the furniture store. *I'm so angry at him,* he raged inside my head. *He has no right to treat you like that, especially when you're trying to help him.*

"Forget about him," I said brightly, even though Heathcliff's callous treatment still smarted. "We'll go talk to Earl and get to the bottom of this. Then Heathcliff will see how much we care for him."

Quoth remained silent. That was good, because I didn't think I could handle him saying that he didn't care about Heathcliff. I put in a call to the store, requesting a new desk to be delivered as soon as possible, then grabbed my gloves and beanie and pushed my way out the front door, bracing myself against the biting cold. Honestly, with the draft turning the shop into an Antarctic blizzard, it wasn't much worse outside.

"Good morning, Mina!" Mrs. Ellis waved at me from across the street. Her granddaughter Jonie huddled under a giant umbrella covered in yellow smiley faces. "Jonie and I are going out for hot chocolate. Do you want to join us?"

"Not right now, I'm afraid. I've got a few chores to do."

Jonie's eyes widened as she stared at Quoth. I noticed she had some bits of tinsel stuck in her hair. *That damn stuff gets everywhere.* "Does your bird just sit on your shoulder like that all day? He doesn't fly away?"

"He could fly away if he wants to," I smiled. Jonie looked to be in a much better mood than the last time I met her. Maybe the Christmas market had done wonders for her mood. "Quoth is my friend. I don't want to force my friend to stay with me. I want him to stay because he enjoys my company."

Her eyes widened even further. "Can I feed him?"

"Sure. I've got some fruit right here…" I reached into my purse, but Jonie dug her hand in her pocket and came up with a handful of birdseed. She held her hand flat and Quoth bent down to gingerly pick the seed from between her fingers.

"Jonie's always got treats on her for animals," Mrs. Ellis smiled. "Her other pocket is filled with doggy biscuits. Deirdre won't let her out of the house until she's thrown the food away, but I think it's good for a child to have interests."

"He's so gentle," Jonie whispered. Behind all that resentment, I could see a true animal lover.

"He is. He's also very intelligent. Some scholars believe ravens have the intellectual abilities of a three-year-old child."

"Croak." Quoth stopped eating to shoot me a filthy look.

I rubbed his head. "Sorry, I meant a four-year-old child."

Jonie's smile could have brightened even Heathcliff. "I wish my mum would let me have a bird. But she'd want it in a cage all the time, and I don't think that's fair."

"Croak," Quoth agreed.

"Do you really want a pet bird?" I asked. "They're really cool, but they can't give you hugs or snuggle at the end of your bed."

I resent that. I give excellent hugs.

"If I could choose any pet, I'd have a dog," Jonie grinned. "A puppy like the ones Mr. Robinson had last night. Then I could train it to do tricks and it would be my best friend. But my mum hates animals. It sucks being a kid when you can't make your own decisions."

"True. It sucks being an adult sometimes, too." I turned to Mrs. Ellis. "Looks like you've got your hands full with this one. Have you seen Earl Larson around this morning, by any chance?"

"Yes. He stopped by the community kitchen this morning, and he was in a jolly mood. Whistlin' Christmas carols and smiling to himself. I suspect he'll be down by the old station. That's where his friends usually gather. Don't be too long now. After we've finished our chocolate we'll be back at Nevermore for some Christmas shopping. I've got my eye on the next *Fifty Shades of Grey* book—"

"I'm afraid you can't. The shop is… closed for repairs." I'd decided not to open the shop so that more villagers could come to gape at the treeless room and gossip about Heathcliff in front of me. It wasn't like we were losing business, anyway – no one wanted to do their shopping with the Argleton Grinch.

Mrs. Ellis' mouth pursed. "Mina, love, you can't let these nasty gossips get to you. Those of us who know Mr. Heathcliff believe in his innocence."

"I appreciate that." I blinked, trying to force back my brimming tears. "But you know how it is – even the police believe he's the thief. They won't dedicate any real resources to finding the stolen gifts, so it's up to me."

"That's horrible," Jonie said, staring at her shoes. I knew she was thinking of all those animals who'd have to go without.

"That's why the shop's shut today – I need to dedicate all my energy to finding the real robber and returning the gifts." I forced a smile for Jonie. "I promise that Quoth and I will find them and all the animals at the shelter will have the best Christmas ever. I'm actually following up a clue right now, so we should get going."

"Thank you, Mina." Mrs. Ellis gave my arm a squeeze as she

and Jonie shuffled toward the bakery. I trudged through the snow in the direction of the old station.

I don't know why you bother defending him, Quoth's voice interrupted my thoughts.

"I know it looks bad," I said aloud. "But we're going to prove his innocence. That's hard to do when even his own friends suspect him."

It's because *I'm his friend that I suspect him,* Quoth said. *You weren't here last Christmas. You haven't seen how he gets. Even by Heathcliff's standards, he's rude and mean and horrible.*

"That's the real mystery," I said. "Why is Heathcliff such a Christmas Grinch? I can tell something's going on with him. He wants to talk about it, but he's afraid. And when he's afraid, he lashes out... Ah, there they are!"

I raced down the street, rounding the corner onto Old Station Road. An old Victorian brick train station house loomed ahead of us, surrounded by piles of rubbish and overgrown weeds. Before I was born the railway had been rerouted to a new station closer to the center of the village to join it up with the main Barchester line, and this station had been abandoned. Every year the village talked about cleaning up the building and turning it into a community center, or a museum, or a garden center. And every year nothing happened. Instead, teens broke inside to drink and smoke and shag, and the local homeless population used it as a shelter and meeting place.

As I approached, I heard the sounds of laughter and singing. I pushed through the station door, but found the building empty of people. Only a few scattered sleeping bags and a billy of water showed anyone had been there. The sounds grew louder as we walked toward the platform.

Quoth peered into the ticketing booth and shook his head. I shoved open one of the broken doors and stepped out onto the platform, stumbling over a long crack in the concrete as I was greeted by a shocking sight.

Earl sat on an upturned rubbish bin, a fiddle pressed to his chin as he played a jaunty reel. Beside him, another homeless guy I recognized from around the village harmonized on a tin whistle. A line of people danced a wild jig around a fire smoldering in an oil drum.

In the center of their revels, towering over the fire like a watchful parent, stood a majestic Christmas tree bedazzled from head to toe with tinsel and glass baubles. It was slightly lopsided with a few broken branches, but otherwise in pristine condition.

It was our tree!

CHAPTER TWELVE

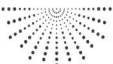

"*H*ey!" I flew into the circle, waving my arms around. "Stop right now!"

Earl's fiddle screeched in protest. Startled by the sound, Quoth flapped wildly, toppling off my shoulder and crashing into the tree. It lurched to the side as the rubbish bin holding it upright struggled with the sudden force. Three people wearing mismatched clothing rushed to right it.

Earl glared at me. "What you doin' here?"

"Why do you think I'm here?" I yelled. "I'm here to have justice for your crime!"

"We was just dancing. That's not illegal."

"I'm talking about the tree! I can't believe you'd steal from us, Earl. I thought you were Heathcliff's friend. The whole village believes Heathcliff stole this tree. They're practically ready to crucify him over it, but it was you all along!"

"I didn't steal this tree!" Earl shot back. "I can't believe you'd suggest such a thing. Mr. Heathcliff gave it to us."

"He did?" That was even worse. That meant that Heathcliff… that he…

Earl nodded. "As good as. He saw me admirin' it through the

83

window the other day, an' he said we could take it after he was done with it. Every year we get the Rose & Wimple tree on December 27th when they take it down, and we have our own Christmas celebration out here, y'see? Only this year's the first year we've been able to have a tree before Christmas! And this one doesn't reek of beer and piss. The kiddies are so happy. That's why we were celebratin'."

"Why did you think Heathcliff was finished with the tree?"

"That woman leaving the shop last night told me Heathcliff said he was done with Christmas. He'd knocked over the tree an' everything. So we figured it was okay for us to take it."

"Why didn't you wait to ask Heathcliff yourself?"

Earl shrugged. His kitten crawled out from the collar of his coat and sat on his shoulder, glaring at Quoth. "You know Mr. Heathcliff, he doesn't much like repeating a conversation if he's already told you once. That an' he's been extra grumpy last couple of weeks. I didn't want to be a bother. I slipped in just after the fella went out, hid in the shadows until she locked up behind her, an' called out to my boys down the street. We wrestled the tree outside an' dragged it down here."

"What about the presents? Don't tell me you've been sharing those around, too?"

Earl shook his head. "We left the presents behind, I swear! Heathcliff never said we could take presents. We may be homeless, Miss Mina, but we don't steal. An' we'd never take someone's Christmas gifts. We know what it's like to have nothin' at Christmas."

Guilt tore at my chest. I was wrong to come here and assume the worst of them. When I saw the tree, I flipped out, but I shouldn't have accused Earl without getting his side of the story first. "I'm sorry, Earl. I shouldn't have made assumptions. I think... I'm scared for Heathcliff, and I left that affect my judgment."

"I'm real sorry, too. We thought it was okay for us to have the tree." Earl snapped his fingers. "Ratty! Boris! Fatso! Get over here. We gotta take the tree back to the bookshop—"

"No. Don't worry about it." I broke into a smile. "Please. I didn't know about the agreement you had with Heathcliff. You keep the tree. We can easily get another one."

"But what about these decorations? They must've cost a pretty penny."

You have no idea. "Keep them, too. I think they look awesome twinkling in the firelight."

"Bless you, Miss Mina." Earl held one of my hands to his chapped lips and kissed my fingers. "You're our Christmas angel."

I didn't feel like a Christmas angel. I felt like complete shit. And we were no closer to figuring out who'd taken the charity gifts. Quoth settled on my shoulder as we trudged along the platform. With trembling fingers, I pulled out my mobile phone and punched in the number of the Kings Copse Wood Christmas Tree Farm.

"Hi, it's Mina Wilde from Nevermore Bookshop. I'd like to order another Christmas tree if you've got any left. Our one was stolen—"

"I'm not selling you another tree just so that rotten Heathcliff can steal it again," the woman on the other end screeched. "Those gifts were for the animals. You should be ashamed of yourselves! Why, I ought to report you to the police for—"

I hung up the phone. Quoth nuzzled my cheek – his feathers soft and warm against my cold skin. *You have to consider this a victory,* he said. *We've found the tree. We have a definite timeline. That's one step closer to identifying our thief.*

"Are you saying you're starting to suspect Heathcliff isn't responsible?" I pushed open the shop door, kicked off my boots, and headed for the staircase.

I think if Heathcliff offered our tree to Earl and his friends so they could have a nice Christmas, then he probably didn't steal gifts meant for the animal shelter.

"I'm glad you think so." I patted Quoth's head. "We've got to remember that we've done this to him before. We assume he's being selfish, but really he's just holding his feelings close to his chest. I bet if we—"

I stopped short, my breath catching in my throat.

No.

It can't be.

But there was no mistaking what I saw. Heathcliff stood in the middle of the living room, trying to shove a large gift-wrapped box into the TV cabinet. There were two smaller presents scattered at his feet, all wrapped in my mother's expensive Bedazzled Bethlehem papers. The look on his face when he saw us was pure guilt and thunder.

Heathcliff did it. He stole the gifts.

CHAPTER THIRTEEN

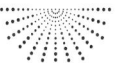

"**G**o away," he growled. "You can't see me like this."

"Heathcliff, what's that package?" I pointed at the box. "That's my mother's wrapping paper – the designs she sold to people for the charity tree."

"It's not."

"It is! And why do you have these gifts?" I bent down to pick up one of the smaller boxes, but Heathcliff snatched it from my hands. "You don't give presents at Christmas, so I know these aren't yours. Why are you hiding them?"

In response, Heathcliff glared at me in stony silence.

"We're out there trying to prove your innocence and..." My hands balled into fists. "I can't believe you really did it."

"You think I stole the presents." Heathcliff's words were clipped, dripping with scorn.

"If you didn't, then why are you trying to hide these from me?" Heathcliff's entire face shut down. "If you'd just talk to me, we could—"

"What's the point in talking? You've already made up your mind." Heathcliff collected the gifts in his arms, stomped from the room, and slammed his bedroom door, shrouding the room in heavy, hurtful silence.

CHAPTER FOURTEEN

I ran downstairs. The furniture guys were just removing the sex desk and dumping out the contents of Heathcliff's drawers in a pile in the corner. I slumped against the wall, my head in my hands. Quoth hopped across the rug in front of me, tugging a string of tinsel for Grimalkin to chase. Even their antics couldn't cheer me up.

At least the furniture guys didn't have any qualms about stepping into the shop owned by Heathcliff the evil Christmas Grinch. The desk's absence left a square of bright blue on the rug, vibrant against the dull grey where the exposed carpet had faded.

A hand rested on my shoulder.

"I don't want to see any more of this moping, gorgeous. We're still working the case." Morrie dragged me to my feet, brushing stray pine needles from the breast of his jacket.

"What's the point? Heathcliff stole the gifts. He won't give them back, and he won't say why he did it."

"Do you really believe that?" Morrie's ice eyes bore into mine. "Do what my arch-nemesis Sherlock Holmes would never do, and put aside the evidence for a moment. You know Heathcliff better than anyone. Would he steal the presents and then hide them right here in the shop?"

I squeezed my eyes shut, bringing up every tender moment and every scorching kiss Heathcliff and I had shared ever since I took the job at Nevermore Bookshop. From our picnic date beside the stream in King's Copse and shagging in the bathroom at Lachlan house to attempting regency dancing at the Jane Austen ball. I'd trod on Heathcliff's feet every few steps, and he never complained. Okay, he did complain. But he never stopped dancing.

"No," I said. "He didn't do it."

"Exactly." Morrie handed me a brand new notebook. "Now let's prove it."

I hunted around in the pile of stationary in the corner for my favorite sparkly pen, but it was still nowhere to be found. Sighing, I picked up another and made a note at the top of the page. "We know Earl and his friends took the tree around 1AM, and the presents were still here. I discovered the presents missing around 7:22AM. That means there's a six-hour window during which the presents could have been stolen. Maybe an intruder snuck in while Earl was leaning out the side window talking to his boys?"

"I'm still betting on the accountant," said Morrie. "I've been tracking him all day. He visited five different shops and businesses in the village and begged them to pay his invoices. He had his dog and her four puppies on a lead, and they're looking very well fed. They all had brand new collars, too. I bet those came from under the tree."

"Princess had five puppies," I corrected him, writing that down.

"Did she? I must've counted wrong." Morrie sounded put out. He didn't like to have his intelligence or observational skills questioned. "Anyway, I think he's our strongest suspect, but he's tricksy. Our only hope of beating him is to catch him red-handed."

"You're probably right. I don't see how we can get him to confess," I said.

"There's always a means." Morrie cracked his knuckles.

"What do you think about Roland Crabapple?" I'd been wondering about the creepy photographer. "He was MIA during our window."

Morrie tapped on his phone. "Interesting that you were thinking about him, too. I was intrigued by something Tabitha said, about him going to King's Copse and video-chatting his cat. So I did some sleuthing on the Dark Web. It turns out our friend the BDSM photographer is a known dendrophiliac."

"What's dendrophilia?" Morrie turned his phone around. At first, all I could see were arty pictures of trees. But then I noticed people in the images as well, hugging the trunks and bending themselves into strange shapes. They were all naked and...

Ew.

Gross.

What?

I shoved his phone away. "I can't unsee that. People are sick."

"Don't be such a prude. Most dendrophiliacs aren't shagging the shrubbery. It's a bit of a mother-earth cult thing, where trees stand as phallic symbolism—"

"Okay, fine, I get it." I held up my hands. "You've painted a vivid picture. So Roland has a tree fetish, which might explain why he wanted to shag Tabitha at the shop or why he might go to King's Copse. But do you think our tree shagger friend would steal the presents?"

Morrie stared at his phone screen, deep in thought. "Roland knew Tabitha had the key. He could have easily slipped it from her pocket and returned it at breakfast. Maybe he got angry when he came back to the shop and found the tree gone, so he decided to steal the presents as a kind of retribution. But I have another explanation – I found this." Morrie handed me his phone again.

I stared at the screen. It was a photograph of a grumpy-looking Persian cat sitting on a throne that looked like something the Romanovs would've turned their noses up at for being too extravagant. I scrolled down. The article was from one of the gossip rags, explaining in lurid detail how Roland was squandering his fortune buying every conceivable luxury for his cat, Miss Purrfect. Apparently, she ate only the finest caviar, had a litter box made of solid gold, and even owned her own Soho penthouse. 'He may be a dominant in the bedroom, but Roland Crabapple has his own master. He's addicted to that cat's approval,' said one source. 'And we all know about cats – it's impossible to truly win their love.'

"All those presents sitting there, going to filthy charity animals when Miss Purrfect was in need?" Morrie remarked. "He had the means and motive."

I circled Roland's name, then Bertie. *Who did it? And how do we find out?* Both of them had a way of getting into the shop, both had a motive, and neither of them seemed like the type to confess their crime just because I asked nicely—

"I've got it!" I cried. "You remember how crazy Grimalkin went over the smell of that catnip spray, even after we cleaned it up? Tabitha said she broke the bottle after she and Roland had finished their... you know. He was already outside the shop when that happened, so he wouldn't have got any on him *unless he came back for the presents*. Whoever stole the presents would reek of the stuff, and I bet it hasn't washed off completely yet. I'll put Grimalkin in my purse and we'll go visit both our suspects. Whichever one she reacts to—"

"—we know that's our Christmas Grinch!" Morrie stood up. "Excellent plan. Now, where is our favorite little thief catcher?"

"Good question." I glanced over at Quoth, who had managed to twist the tinsel string around his wing, and was frantically trying to flap it off. Grimalkin was nowhere in sight. "Where's Grimalkin?"

"Croak."

"Well, didn't you see where she went?"

"Croak."

"You're no good." I stood up and peered under the table. She wasn't there, nor was she skulking along the top of the poetry bookshelf, nor had she busied herself in the boxes of secondhand stock at the back of Heathcliff's office – her favorite spot to hide decapitated rodents. "Grimalkin, here kitty, kitty…"

"Meow."

I spun around just as a flash of black darted through the hall-way, trailing a tail of bright tinsel behind her.

"Meow!" Grimalkin called happily, her feet skidding on the wooden floor as she dragged Quoth's tinsel behind her.

"No, Grimalkin, come back with that!" I scurried after her, Morrie hot on my heels. Grimalkin assumed it was a game and poured on speed, ducking and weaving between the shelves to confuse us before dragging her prize through a narrow gap behind the Natural History shelves. I bent down to peer inside, and a blast of cold air hit me square in the face.

"What's this?" I asked Morrie.

He frowned into the gap. "Odd. The cellar door is behind that shelf. But it's locked. There shouldn't be a breeze. Congratula-tions, gorgeous. You've found the source of the shop's mysterious draft."

"But how is there a draft where there are no windows or entrances in the cellar?" I shoved the end of the bookcase. "Help me with this. If Grimalkin's gone down there, we have to find her."

Morrie dropped his shoulder against the wood and shoved. Luckily, this particular bookcase was on wheels, and it slid aside easily so we could access the cellar's latch. I flitted it open to reveal rickety stone steps leading down into a black hole.

I slid my phone out of my pocket and flipped on the flashlight app. Frigid air screamed up the stairs and blasted my bare face. After a few steps, even the flashlight beam was useless. Down here it was so dark, I was completely blind.

"Grimalkin, where are you?"

I kept my hand pressed against the wall and used my feet to feel for the next step. Cold air rushed up. I could hear Grimalkin chattering away, but she sounded muffled, like she was trapped in a cupboard or something.

I yelled up the stairs. "Morrie, help!"

A few moments later, footsteps clattered on the stairs. "The Napoleon of Crime to the rescue," Morrie purred in my ear, wrapping his arms around my body and kissing along my neck.

"As tempting as you are, it's too cold for your shenanigans." My teeth chattered. I pressed my phone into his hand. "Grimalkin's down here somewhere, chewing up my tinsel. Can you find her? I can't see."

By Isis, I *hated* asking for help. I hated that I couldn't do something. But my feelings weren't important right now. We had to find Grimalkin. It might be dangerous down here, and I didn't want her to crawl into some tight space and become stuck.

"Of course." Morrie shone the phone around the gloomy space. "Here, kitty, kitty…"

Grimalkin responded with a defiant, "Meow!"

"Ah. I see tinsel." Morrie lunged into the darkness.

BANG. CRASH.

"Meorrrrrrrrw!"

"What's going on?" I squinted, but I couldn't make out anything except the beam of light swinging wildly.

"It's fine!" Morrie panted. "I've got everything under control —argh!"

CLATTER! CRASH!

"What happened?" I surged forward, my hands in front of my

face to feel for obstacles as I fought my way through centuries of spiderwebs to reach Morrie.

"I caught Grimalkin's tail, but she scratched me and I sort of… fell through the wall. It must've been thin here—hang on a second…" There were a few more clatters and thumps, and then a warm hand circled my wrist. Morrie pulled me close as a frigid draft screamed past us. "Mina, there's a tunnel behind the wall."

"What?"

"A tunnel. It's where the draft's coming in. There was a small hole in the corner, just big enough for a little cat to fit in and… well, looky here." Morrie swung the beam into the mouth of the tunnel.

"Morrie, *what?*"

"Go on. Guess."

"I hope you're not mocking the visually impaired, because I'm not in the mood. Tell me what you see."

"It's all the small stuff that's gone missing from the shop over the last couple of weeks. Your sparkly pen. Your hair clips. A couple of your mother's expensive baubles. It looks like you're not the only one who loves sparkles."

"Oh, Grimalkin." I couldn't help but grin. I loved that crazy cat.

"This is wild." Morrie held up the treasures under the light. Glitter sparkled as my mother's baubles and several of my favorite bobby pins came into view. "We have a real-life cat burglar in our midst. It makes me wonder if Grimalkin was the one who took the presents."

"Meow?" Grimalkin batted at Morrie's arm, as if to say, 'hands off my treasure.'

"That's impossible." I rubbed Grimalkin between the ears until she purred.

Morrie shone the flashlight back into the hole. "Maybe, but I think we might have another idea of how our burglar entered the shop. In the corner of the panel is a board that's nearly rotted away, where Grimalkin was squeezing through. Now I've broken the whole thing, I can see it's a door fitted on a spring. You can open it from the inside and out. This has probably been here for centuries and we never knew about it."

"That's so cool." I shoved my pilfered belongings into my pocket and gripped his shoulder. "Help me in. We've got to see where it leads."

Good old Morrie. It never occurred to him to question if it was a good idea for us to explore a dark and possibly dangerous tunnel without telling anyone else what we were doing (spoiler alert: it wasn't). He fitted my hand into the crook of his arm and steadied me as I felt for each step with my feet. "I'm stooping because the ceiling's low," he said. "But you should be fine to stand up straight."

"Thanks, Morrie." We shuffled down the passage, the thin beam of light from both our phones illuminating stone walls slick with damp. Above our heads, the cold air rushed in from a vent that must connect with the street above, judging by the tiny grey shaft of light it cast on the ground.

"Watch your head," Morrie said, just as my forehead smacked into a low arch.

"Thanks for the warning," I muttered, rubbing my head.

Water dribbled down the brick walls, and my boots crunched on ice formed between the stones. *What a miserable place.*

"This stone looks old," Morrie said. "This tunnel could have been part of a drainage system for the village, or a secret passage for smugglers, or it could be connected somehow to the time-traveling room."

Another of Nevermore Bookshop's uncanny secrets.

It didn't take long until we reached the other end of the tunnel. My foot kicked something on the floor. I picked it up and felt it in my hands. It was a stainless steel dish – the kind you'd give a dog for water or food.

"There's stairs here," Morrie led me up narrow stone steps.

The wall on one side of us turned from stone to wood, and I had the sense we were moving between the walls of a house.

There was a click as Morrie popped open another door. We stepped out into a bright room. I blinked, and in a few moments my eyes had adjusted enough to make out the space.

We were in a bedroom – small with a low ceiling, but comfortable. The walls were painted pastel yellow and covered with posters of cats and puppies and pop stars. An overflowing suitcase at the end of the bed spilled clothes across the floor, and a stack of books on the nightstand showed the room's inhabitants had a thing for YA vampire fiction.

But that wasn't the most extraordinary thing about the room. On every surface were stacked bright colored boxes and parcels tied with bows. Gifts of all shapes and sizes, many of them opened and the contents raided. I picked up a gift tag and flipped it over to read the message written in a child's loopy handwriting.

DEAR ANIMALS OF ARGLETON. I HOPE YOU FIND SAFE HOMES FOR CHRISTMAS. LOVE ARTHUR.

The presents from our Christmas tree. We'd found them. But who had taken them—

"You shouldn't be here," a voice said.

"Arf!" added another voice.

My heart leaped in my throat. The thieves were right behind us!

I whirled around just as a figure stepped into the room.

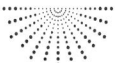

CHAPTER FIFTEEN

The shadow advanced, arms outstretched. It let out an inhuman yowl that chilled my bones. Was it even human? Had we come face-to-face with a dark nightmare from an HP Lovecraft storybook—

"Jonie?" I gasped as the figure came into view. In her arms, she held a tiny golden retriever puppy with the biggest, roundest brown eyes. The puppy whimpered. "Arf?" it asked weakly.

Jonie didn't even acknowledge us. She set down the dog in a brand-new bed, patting its matted fur. "Here you go, Buster. I know they scared you, but it's okay. I've got some treats here to make it all better." She plunged her hand into one of the gift boxes and pulled out a bag of dog treats, which she tipped on the rug. The puppy, Buster, sniffed at the treats, then turned his head away. His tail flapped a couple of times. He looked sick.

"Jonie, you stole the presents from under the Christmas tree." I couldn't believe it. "You love animals. Why would you want to hurt them like this?"

Jonie slumped on the bed, wiping at her eyes. It took me a moment to realize she was crying.

"I know what I did was wrong," she sniffed. "I was going to

pay for new presents, so none of the animals would have missed out. Grandma always gives me a check for Christmas. I would use the money to replace all the toys and food so none of the animals would have missed out. But Buster needed things *now*. I don't have any money, and I couldn't ask Mum for it because she's in Paris and doesn't want to talk to me."

I sat down beside Jonie, starting to put together what might've happened. "Where did you get Buster?"

"From Bertie – that weird guy with the tiny glasses." The puppy slumped at Jonie's feet. She pulled him onto the bed, where he rested his head on her lap. She stroked him, her face brightening into a smile. "I met him when he came to ask my Grandma about the accounts for the Christmas market. He said he'd give Buster to me for free if I could feed him and keep him healthy. So I snuck through the tunnel and took the presents, and then Bertie let me take Buster home after the market. I've been such a good mama to him! I fed him and played with him and given him lots of snuggles. The only time I can't be with him is when Grandma's home – I have to hide him in the tunnel. Today I even tried to take him out for a walk. But he's so sad. He just sits in that bed and he won't eat and I don't know what to do!"

I remembered Bertie talking with Jonie at the fete. He gave her one of the puppies. I thought she was just having a cuddle, but she must've taken him home. I rubbed my hands together, trying to get feeling into my numb fingers. *If the puppy was stuck in that tunnel for any length of time, no wonder he's feeling sick.*

Josie buried her head in her hands and bawled.

"I knew I didn't count wrong," Morrie cried in triumph. "The accountant only had four puppies today because the fifth one was here."

Not the time, I mouthed at him as I sat down beside Jonie and wrapped my arms around her.

"I couldn't say no!" Jonie picked up Buster and cradled him to her chest. "Look at his face! Besides, Bertie couldn't take care of

Buster. He said so himself. He was going to abandon Buster and his brothers and sisters at the animal shelter. I knew that with so many animals needing homes over Christmas, they'd be unlikely to find a new family in time. I *had* to help him." Tears streaked her face. "Am I in trouble?"

"You tried to do a good thing, Jonie. But you stole things that were meant for others and lied about it. You let everyone in the village believe Heathcliff had taken the tree and presents. That *was* wrong. Why didn't you tell your grandma about Buster? She would have helped you pay for his food and supplies. Wouldn't that be better than stealing?"

"I didn't tell her because I'm not allowed to have a pet." Jonie sighed, slumping down on the bed. "Grandma Mabel would tell my mum and I'd get into so much trouble. Mum won't let me have a pet because she wants her new boyfriend to move in and he hates dogs. Of course he does. He hates anything I like because he hates me, even if I try so hard to be good and do what they want and not bother them while they're on their dates. But it was so cold out and Bertie didn't even have a coat on Buster, and he's just a tiny puppy. I think he was sick even then. I couldn't just leave him."

Jonie's tear-streaked face broke my heart. Of course, she felt neglected by her mother. I would too if I'd been shuffled off to stay with my grandma over the holidays so Mum could go to Paris with her dog-hating boyfriend.

I thought of my oddball mother and all her insane shenanigans. Even though she drove me crazy with her wacky ideas and insane pyramid schemes, she really did love me. She'd never ship me off out of her way so she could be with a guy. "Any bloke I like enough to bring home has to be able to handle both Wilde women," she used to tell me whenever I asked her why she didn't have a boyfriend. "So far, no one has come close."

Buster whimpered again, and his tiny body trembled.

"Can I have a look at him?" I reached for the puppy. Reluctantly, Jonie passed him over. Buster's eyes drooped, and he whined when I touched him. He flattened his ears against his head. I knew that animals often hid how sick they were until it was too late.

My suspicions were confirmed when I held him. He was a bag of skin and bones, and even though he was wearing a woolly sweater, he trembled in my arms. Buster's pupils weren't just large – they were dilated. His skin felt cold, and when he drooped his head and touched his nose to my arm, the cold of it shocked me.

"Jonie, I think he's really sick. We need to take him to the vet right now."

Fresh tears welled in Jonie's eyes. "It's all my fault. I tried to take care of him. Every time I love someone, they leave me. Dad walked out. Mum went to Paris. I can't even keep a dog alive."

I squeezed her leg as I scooped Buster into my arms. "It's not your fault. I'm sure you've taken good care of him. I'm sure everything will be okay."

Please, please let everything be okay.

CHAPTER SIXTEEN

*M*orrie called a rideshare and we rushed Buster over to the vet clinic. Jonie broke down in the waiting room, sobbing into Morrie's shoulder while I sat in on the consultation. As I suspected, Buster had hypothermia, probably from being hidden in that freezing secret tunnel.

The vet wrapped Buster in warm blankets and placed him on a heating pad. He set up an IV to help warm Buster recover. "You're lucky you caught this when you did," he told me. "Hypothermia can be as dangerous for dogs as it is in people. I'm going to do some blood tests to make sure there's no long-term damage, but I believe Buster is going to be just fine."

While we waited with Jonie for the tests, I called DS Wilson and told her where she could find the presents. "Mrs. Ellis is either at her knitting circle or her BDSM for seniors group... I hope for your sake it's the former. Get her to help you collect them all from Jonie's room. If you drop them back at the bookshop, I'll see that they're re-wrapped and a replacement tree located."

"Will do." DS Wilson paused. "Mina, I should apologize to Heathcliff, and to you. I made assumptions—"

"I know," I said. "Me, too."

I hung up the phone. DS Wilson wasn't the only one who needed to apologize. My stomach twisted in knots – I hated that Heathcliff was out there thinking I doubted him. It would do no good to call him, since the lovable curmudgeon didn't even own a mobile phone. I'd already tried the shop. Quoth picked up and said Heathcliff wasn't there.

Where can he be?

Ah, of course. He's gone to King's Copse.

Heathcliff may spend most of his time cooped up in the book-shop, but he was still a wild man at heart. The moors ran in his veins. There were no moors near Argleton, but there *was* a hidden stream in the King's Copse wood where we had our first real date. If Heathcliff was upset, he'd go there.

I yanked my coat off the seat and raced for the door, already punching in a request on my rideshare app. I could still get to the wood and back before the vet was finished with Buster and—

My body crashed into something hard.

A wall?

Walls weren't warm. Or wearing coats with torn black fur fringe.

Heathcliff.

My breath caught in my throat.

"I heard about the puppy," he said, his voice gruff. "Is he all right?"

That did it. I fell into his arms, letting him sweep me up into one of those hugs that drove the air from my lungs. "I'm so sorry. I never should have doubted you. I believed you until I saw you hiding those presents and I… I let the detective in me take over, instead of listening to the girlfriend."

"It's okay," he said gruffly, his huge hands running circles on my back.

"It's not okay," I sniffed. "You're my boyfriend and I love you. Your word should have been enough for me to trust you."

"Why? I gave you every reason to mistrust me." Heathcliff stroked my hair. "If things had been reversed, I might've wrestled with the same questions."

I pulled back. "Heathcliff, why do you hate Christmas so much?"

He stiffened. "It's because of… before."

"In your fiction life?"

He nodded. "Cathy stayed at Thrushcross Grange until Christmas. When I left her, she was my wild woman, but when she returned she had all these airs and manners and fine clothes and a haughty attitude. While she'd been gone, there was no one to shield me from the family's neglect and tortures. Nobody but Nelly even did me the kindness to speak to me during that wretched time. I lived mostly outdoors, foraging for my food and sleeping with the horses, and so when she returned, I was befouled with mire and dust – a forbidding blackguard next to her bright and graceful beauty. Hindley relished my discomfort. When the Lintons called on Cathy, Nelly helped me to make myself presentable and I swore to be good, but Hindley's scorn and my own nature betrayed me. Hindley and that goat Linton mocked me, and for defending myself from their insults I was banished from the room."

I nodded. I remembered well that chapter of *Wuthering Heights*. Catherine at the table, cutting her goose wing and engaging in lively talk with the Lintons, with no thought to Heathcliff confined to the garret. Later, she snuck in to see him, and when she dragged him back to the kitchen, he'd told Nelly that the only time he didn't feel pain was when he was thinking of the satisfaction he would feel upon punishing those who wronged him.

"Christmas became an ill omen – it had changed Cathy forever. She'd been stolen away by the fairies and returned as one of them. She was forever remote and beyond my reach, and she knew it. She tormented me with it, for she alone could love me and hurt me like no one else. All these songs about Christmas being magical – they're right. But it's a dark and foul magic. Christmas changes people – it makes them forget who they are. I swore it would never change me – I would never succumb to its spell."

"But you *have* changed." I wiped a tear from the corner of my eye. "Maybe it's not Christmas magic at all, but something inside you has been broken open and remade anew. You're not that same cold and bitter boy anymore."

"That's not Christmas magic." Heathcliff pressed his lips to mine. "It's you, Mina. Cathy made me want to burn the world. You make me want to be a better person."

My chest swelled at his words, only to be crushed by the fury of his lips. Heathcliff's kiss consumed me utterly, for with his lips and tongue he expressed a longing deep and fearsome and beautiful – he gave himself to me utterly, a promise that if all else perished and he remained, I would continue to be. To be loved by Heathcliff, to be kissed by him, was to have our souls become one.

Everything made sense now – Heathcliff's sullen mood, his resistance to having anything Christmassy in the shop, his refusal to exchange gifts. But then… "What about those presents you were hiding?"

"I guess it's time you found out." Heathcliff leaned over and produced a faded rucksack from behind the chair. He unzipped it and pulled out a gift-wrapped box. "I got this for you."

I held it in my arms, awed by the existence of it. It was the gift I'd seen him trying to hide in the TV cabinet. The gift tag bore my name. Heathcliff, who had sworn an oath that he wouldn't participate in Christmas, had gotten me a gift.

"This is the box you were trying to hide from me," I breathed.

He nodded. "I was going to surprise you with it on Christmas day. I was trying to find a way to tell you that I was letting go of the old Heathcliff, the one who hated Christmas because of my ex-girlfriend. I wanted you to see that I was trying to see Christmas the way you do. It was in my room when DS Wilson asked to search it. You were standing right there. I didn't want to spoil the surprise. So I was going to move it to the TV cabinet and let you look in my room, but then you saw me."

And I'd thrown his efforts back in his face. Shame squirmed inside me. "I'm so, so sorry."

"Enough of that." Heathcliff tapped the box. "Open it."

I tore off the expensive wrapping paper. Inside was a plain cardboard box, dented on one side, probably from Heathcliff trying to shut the cabinet door on it. I slid my finger under the tape and pried the lid off.

Inside was an amazing pink-and-black leopard-print faux-fur blanket. When I drew it out into the light, beams of color leapt off dazzling sequins and a sparkling ribbon border. It was the most punk rock blanket I'd ever seen.

"Wow." I held it to my cheek, relishing the softness.

"I won it in the Christmas pub quiz. You've been complaining about the cold in the shop, so I thought you could use something to help keep warm," Heathcliff muttered. "Turns out I could have just plugged the hole Grimalkin made in the cellar door and it would've caused less trouble."

"Heathcliff, it's perfect." I threw my arms around him again. "I love it. And I love *you*. Merry Christmas."

He grunted in reply. I guessed some things never change.

An idea occurred to me. I turned to the others. "We can't do anything more for Buster tonight. What do you guys say we go over to the Rose & Wimple and hit up Richard's famous Christmas roast?"

"Sounds good, but is it a good idea to go out in public?" Quoth asked. "What if people haven't heard we have all the presents back?"

"Then we'll just have to tell them the true story. Besides," I grinned. "I have a brilliant idea for how Heathcliff can win back the affections of the town."

Heathcliff stiffened, his dark eyes narrowing with suspicion. "Why do I have the feeling I'm not going to like this?"

CHAPTER SEVENTEEN

*B*uster the puppy needed to spend the day and night under observation at the vet clinic, but finally, he was given a clean bill of health. I woke up at the crack of dawn on Christmas morning to go with Jonie to pick him up. Quoth decided to come along.

As I passed through the shop on the way out the door, I couldn't help but feel a tinge of sadness. When I hadn't been helping customers find last-minute gifts at the shop, I'd spent every spare moment over the last day with Jonie at the clinic. I hadn't had time to shop for food or even source a new tree. All the presents for the animal shelter were stacked in a towering heap in the corner. Grimalkin had torn down most of the decorations on her catnip high. The place didn't feel very festive. My dreams of a perfect Nevermore Christmas were just that – dreams.

At least it's snowing outside, Quoth reminded me. *You love snow. Maybe we'll have that snowball fight later.*

He was right, of course. Snowflakes tickled my nose as I made my way across the street to Mrs. Ellis' flat. The whole of Argleton looked like the front of a Christmas card. The bakery piped

Christmas carols into the street through a tinny speaker, and delicious smells wafted in the air from all directions.

"Merry Christmas, Quoth!" Jonie cried as she skipped out of the flat with a handful of berries for Quoth. "Merry Christmas, Mina!"

Mrs. Ellis called a rideshare and we made it to the vet, who had opened the clinic just for us. When she emerged carrying the bright-eyed pup in her arms, we all clapped. The smile on Jonie's face could have lit a black hole.

"You won't believe it!" Jonie cried. "Mum called me this morning from Paris. She said that I could keep Buster as long as I agreed to be responsible for walking and feeding and training him. It's the best Christmas present ever!"

Over Jonie's shoulder, Mrs. Ellis winked at me. I suspect she'd had something to do with her daughter's change of heart.

I hugged Jonie. "That's wonderful news. I know you're going to be an amazing friend to Buster."

"Croak," Quoth agreed.

The rideshare dropped us at the top of Butcher Street and we said a brief goodbye to Jonie and Mrs. Ellis at their front door. They were going to pick up a lead and some treats for Buster, then meet us at the shop. Even though we didn't have a tree and I hadn't purchased any Christmas food, we were all going to celebrate together.

I walked in the door, and was immediately knocked about the head with an amazing smell.

Mmmmm... hot toddies... and Christmas mince pies fresh from the oven, and pigs in blankets, and is that the sound of a Champagne cork popping?

"Hot stuff, coming through!" Morrie swung down the staircase in a Santa apron, holding a platter of Christmas goodies. He winked at Quoth and dashed into the main room.

"What's going on?" I asked Quoth.

He shrugged his wings. "Croak?"

A lump rose in my throat as I followed Morrie into the main room. I gasped. In the short time we'd been gone, the space had been transformed. A respectable-sized tree stood in the window, decked out with strings of tinsel and a few glass baubles. Underneath it, presents stacked as high as the windowsill – all the charity gifts from the town neatly arranged. Morrie stood behind Heathcliff's brand new desk, pouring Champagne into flutes and fussing over a dazzling array of treats – bowls of sweets and chocolate reindeer, crackers and cheese. A small pile of gifts I didn't recognize from the charity lay at the front of the tree. As I bent to examine the scrawled labels, my heart skipped.

TO THE ANNOYING BIRD

TO THE WORLD'S WORST ENTREPRENEUR

TO THE NOSY OLD BIDDY

TO MY OBNOXIOUS FLATMATE

Across the bottom of each tag was a familiar and wonderful scrawl. FROM HEATHCLIFF.

He did this. He made Christmas for me.

I knelt back, tears of joy pooling in my eyes as I searched the room for Heathcliff. A dark figure crouched by the fire. I couldn't believe I hadn't seen him when I walked in, but I'd been so distracted by everything. He blew on the logs and stood back. A warming fire roared to life.

"Heathcliff." I threw myself in his arms.

"It's no fuss," he muttered. But he pulled me closer, his lips finding mine for a scorching, possessive kiss. A kiss that promised my Christmas treats had only just begun.

I pulled back to catch my breath and wipe my eyes. "This is amazing. How did you do all this?"

"It's not a big thing. While you were running around after that dog yesterday, I walked over to the tree place and chose a sensibly-sized tree, carried it home, and hid it in the office. We're never going to get rid of the needles in there now, but I've decided to just close the door and never enter until next bloody

Christmas. I gave Morrie some money to take care of the food. We didn't have time to buy decorations, but I salvaged those ones from the cat." Heathcliff nodded at the tinsel on the tree. A rare, genuine smile lit up his gruff face. "Do you like it?"

My voice cracked. "I love it. I—"

"Yoohoo, Merry Christmas." Mum walked in, laden down with a stack of presents and a box of her Bedazzling Bethlehem decorations. "Oh, look at that poor empty tree. Luckily, I've got lots of things to brighten it up." She started pulling out all kinds of sparkling things.

"Champagne, Helen?" Morrie held out two flutes.

"Don't mind if I do. Mina, come help me with these decorations."

Reluctantly, I let go of Heathcliff and collected my flute from Morrie. Mum had found a tiny Santa hat in the stack and perched it on Quoth's head. "Mum, what are you going to do with all those boxes of decorations now Christmas is over?"

Mum beamed at me. She dug a pamphlet out of her pocket and thrust it under my face. "I thought you might want them to enter this! It's this World of Wearable Arts Award in New Zealand. I saw it on the telly. People make these amazing costumes and wear them on stage and there are tens of thousands of dollars in prize money. There's a whole category for sparkling and glowing costumes, so I figured that would be perfect for you—"

"That does sound very cool, but why would I enter something like that? I told you I'm not continuing with fashion. I love my job—"

"Oh, Mina, you can't work in this stuffy bookshop forever." Mum leaned forward, her eyes dancing. "Unless... you don't think Morrie will go in for a Christmas proposal?"

I choked on my mouthful of Champagne. Bubbles shot up my nose. Behind me, Heathcliff snorted. Morrie, thankfully, was in the hallway greeting Mrs. Ellis and Jonie, and hadn't heard her.

I hadn't *officially* told Mum that I was dating all three guys. I hadn't been hiding it, but in typical Mum fashion she chose to see what she wanted, which was that I was madly in love with rich, successful Morrie, who would sweep me off my feet in a whirlwind romance, marry me, and then keep his mother-in-law in the fashionable manner to which she intended to become accustomed.

I snatched the pamphlet from her hand. "What? Mum, *no*. And don't suggest it, either. I'm not ready to get married."

Especially since I had three boyfriends and I couldn't marry all of them.

"Nonsense! You're young and in love, and Morrie is perfect for you." Mum dug around in her box, pulling out something green and waving it about in triumph. "Ah-hah! I knew I had some mistletoe in here. I'm going to go hang this over the door. Then Morrie won't have a choice but to make his move."

"Mum, please—" But it was too late. She trotted off, trailing a string of mistletoe behind her.

After drinks and snacks were handed out, we gathered around the fire and exchanged gifts. Quoth presented me with the most beautiful painting – a portrait of me sitting in the velvet chair, reading a stack of my favorite books while a row of white skulls grinned down at me from the shelf above. I immediately made Heathcliff bang a nail in the office wall so we could hang it up. Quoth beamed to see how much I loved it, and his smile burned brighter than all the Christmas lights in the shop.

Morrie handed me my own cell phone. "I've installed a new app for you." He pointed to the icon. It was an audiobook store, and he'd already loaded my account with enough money to keep me in books for a year. I could listen to my favorite authors while I stacked the shelves. I immediately downloaded *Shunned* by Steffanie Holmes and started listening.

My chest fluttered with nerves as I passed around my presents. They were all the same size and shape and went to everyone in the room. When I'd finished them up last night and wrapped them for under the tree, I'd felt quietly confident that I'd found the perfect gift for all the people I loved most. Now, I was having second thoughts. As Heathcliff took the parcel in his hands, I fought the sudden urge to snatch it back.

"What's this?" Heathcliff tore off the wrapping to reveal a sheaf of papers. "Are you going to use this to bludgeon me until I agree to be on the cloud?"

"*How Heathcliff Stole Christmas.*" Morrie read the title aloud from his copy. "Mina, what is this?"

My cheeks burned with heat. "It's a story. I wrote up the mystery of the stolen tree and how we solved it. I thought…"

I couldn't finish the sentence. I didn't know what I was thinking. I'd typed out the story in a fit of excitement over the last few days, late at night while sitting at Heathcliff's desk and on my phone while I waited at the vet clinic. Now, in the warm light of the fire, with six pairs of eyes staring back at me, I felt a complete fool. *What a dumb Christmas present. Why would they want to read my ramblings? I should have just gone with the Dutch chocolate ravens...*

Morrie's eyes widened as he flicked through the pages. "This is amazing. And hilarious. You've spent at least three paragraphs describing how handsome I am. I approve."

"Mina, I had no idea you could write." Mum flicked through her 'clean' copy – there was a certain scene that appeared only in the guys' manuscripts. "

"She was always my star pupil," Mrs. Ellis declared, turning the pages eagerly. "I hope there's lots of raunchy parts."

"Look at the dedication," Heathcliff whispered, his knuckles white as he gripped the pages.

Beside me, Quoth's eyes darted across the paper. "To the men of Nevermore," he read aloud, his voice trembling over the words. "It has made me better loving you … it has made me wiser, and easier, and brighter."

"That's from Henry James," I muttered. I'd written and rewritten that bloody dedication a hundred times in my own words but nothing seemed sufficient. I thought the words of one of my favorite writers might accurately convey my feelings for the guys.

Quoth threw his arms around me. "This is the most beautiful thing anyone has ever done for me."

Morrie bent down and swept me into a fiery kiss. "It's pretty great, gorgeous. You have a hidden talent for slinging words. Maybe there's a creative career in your future yet."

Heathcliff's dark eyes bore into mine. He swallowed hard and opened his mouth to speak, but he didn't say a thing. Instead, he tore me from Morrie's grasp and devoured my lips with his. In his kiss, he said all the things that words were impossible to convey.

My heart fluttered at their praise and acceptance. I'd wanted so badly for them to like my gift, to understand that by bringing me into their world they'd given me the greatest gift of all. I wanted them to see how wonderful they were through my eyes.

After everyone finished reading and exclaiming over my story, Heathcliff handed out small wrapped boxes to Morrie and Quoth. He then removed a small envelope from his pocket and held it out to me.

I stared down at the envelope in his hand. "You already gave me a gift."

"Maybe I'm making up for previous infractions." He tapped the envelope in my hand. "Open it."

I slid my nail under the seal. Inside was a Christmas card covered with dancing sheep in Santa hats. It said, "Seasons Bleatings," which was totally more of a Morrie joke, but I'd give Heathcliff credit for originality. Inside was a folded paper covered in tiny writing. I held it up to the light and squinted at the words.

It was the deed to the shop.

"Look." Heathcliff jabbed a finger at the top paragraph. "Bertie helped me draw it up. I had to give him a massive bonus to finish it on Christmas Eve, so he's the happiest accountant you ever saw. There's your name, all nice and proper. We're now co-owners of Nevermore Bookshop."

My name. All I had to do was sign on the line and Nevermore belonged to me. Heathcliff had given me the best gift of all – a future. A home.

Morrie leaned over my shoulder and whistled. "That's hardly fair. Even my app can't top that. I'm going to give you the deed to a real castle next year. Maybe that fancy Briarwood property near Crookshollow. Let's see the Earl of Dour-ton Abbey top *that.*"

I smiled at the gift box in Morrie's hand. It was one of the boxes Heathcliff had been trying to hide. "What did you get?"

Grinning, Morrie held up an engraved silver keychain shaped like a book. "Mine says, 'World's most annoying criminal.' Quoth got one, too. His has a line from 'The Raven.' And both of them include a brand new key for the flat. Our Grand Old Duke of Sourpuss is quite good at this Christmas thing."

He was at that.

"I love you boys like you were my own sons. And Mina, you are like a daughter who doesn't run away to Paris on Christmas." Mrs. Ellis was on her fourth flute of Champagne. Her cheeks glowed pink as she leaned forward to pat Buster's head. "I'm so sorry again Jonie caused you all that trouble. But thanks to you, another mystery has been solved."

"Except for a few loose ends to wrap up," I pointed out as Quoth hopped off my shoulder and fluttered upstairs. "We still don't know where Roland went during the night. Or why the bauble was in the hallway upstairs."

"I must've had all those baubles and shite stuck to my clothes when I knocked over the tree," Heathcliff said. "I was trying to wrap your present with those poxy supplies your mum left lying around, but everything was so fiddly and complicated, and I was too drunk. I dragged everything upstairs and dumped it in my room to figure out in the morning. That bauble must've come along for the ride."

"As for Roland, I can answer that." Morrie held up his phone. "It looks like our favorite tree-loving photographer made a little midnight jaunt into Kings Copse wood. He's just uploaded a series of time-stamped photos to a dendrophilia website. Here, look—"

"That's okay." I shoved the phone away. "I think I've seen just enough of Roland dancing skyclad under trees. What about Bertie? Did you find out why he came back to the shop?"

"He really *did* just collect the tax forms from last quarter. He returned our accounts ledger this morning." Heathcliff thumped the thick leather-bound book sitting on his brand-new desk. "Apparently, we're due a significant tax refund. I thought I might use some of it to purchase a permanent supply of Christmas decorations for the shop."

I grinned. "Or it could go toward a cloud accounting system—"

"Or I could find a new accountant who won't hassle me about cloud accounting," Heathcliff shot back.

"Arf!" Buster's ears flattened. His tiny paws churned as he immediately careened off into the shelves after Grimalkin.

"I'm so glad to see Buster's doing well," I grinned.

Instead of answering me, Jonie flung herself at Heathcliff, wrapping her arms around his torso.

"What's it doing?" Heathcliff demanded, staring down at the child in disbelief.

"I think it likes you," Morrie said.

"Then it's a bloody fool."

"I'm sorry, Mr. Heathcliff. I should have come forward and told the truth." Jonie buried her face in his coat.

"S'okay." Heathcliff stared at his hands.

"I didn't mean for everyone to hate you, especially not your friends. I know what it feels like to be rejected by the people you love. I hope you can forgive me."

Heathcliff patted her head like she was a dog. That was the closest he'd probably be able to get to expressing his affection for Jonie. They really were both quite alike.

Quoth shuffled into the room in his human form, his tentative steps bringing him to Heathcliff. He stared up at his friend with wide eyes, then threw his own arms around Heathcliff's neck. "I'm sorry, too."

"It's okay, birdie." Heathcliff tried to pry Quoth's fingers from around his neck, but Quoth was used to hanging on tight.

"I'm not going to miss out on the fun." Morrie threw himself into the group hug. Grimalkin leaped from the Poetry shelf and sank her claws into Heathcliff's shoulder. Mum helped Mrs. Ellis to her feet so they could squeeze in. Jonie grabbed Buster from the floor and the two of them joined in, piling on Heathcliff until he was just a stony face in the middle of a huddle of love.

Grinning from ear to ear, I stepped forward and enveloped them all. My three wonderful, wild, crazy, enchanting boyfriends who made every day so special – especially Christmas. My mother, who drove me crazy but who was also amazing. And Mrs. Ellis and Jonie, who had wheeled their way into all our hearts. I couldn't be happier to be sharing this Christmas with them.

"Who pinched my arse?" Heathcliff growled.

Morrie grinned. "Guilty."

I laughed. Having all of us together like this – that was what *really* made Christmas the most wonderful time of the year. The magic of Christmas wasn't in the food or the carols or the decorations – it was the people.

Although… the food and booze and blazing fire sure helped.

Morrie glanced up, his brow furrowed. "Mina, why is your mother holding a bunch of leaves over my head?"

"It's mistletoe. She thinks she's going to push you into proposing to me." I glared at my mother, who only beamed in return.

"I could propose if you like." Morrie's tongue danced across my earlobe. "I propose we drag Heathcliff into that supply cupboard over there, and the two of us can stuff your stocking while you ride us like a reindeer—"

"Morrie!" I slapped his arm. "We've got no time for that. It's almost noon. We've got somewhere important to be."

"That's right!" Morrie slapped his forehead. "I nearly forgot."

"I wish you had," Heathcliff muttered.

A slow, happy smile spread across Quoth's face as he, too, remembered what I had planned next.

I planted both hands on Heathcliff's shoulders and shoved him toward the door. "No arguments. If you want to know about the true meaning of Christmas, you're going to come with me, and you're going to like it."

"I'm good not knowing, actually—" But Heathcliff's protests fell on deaf ears as I dragged him out into the snow.

"Heathcliff Earnshaw, you've given me the best Christmas I've ever had, and I love you like mad for it. Now, allow me to return the favor and give you a Christmas you'll never forget. Come *on*, we don't want to keep your public waiting."

EPILOGUE

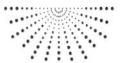

"*D*o I have to do this?" Heathcliff grumbled.

"Yes." I gave him a shove toward the door.

"They'll eat me alive."

"They're more afraid of you than you are of them." I paused, watching as children at the front of the line trembled with fright. *Okay, maybe not.* "Anyway, that's not the point. If you want the village to love you again—"

"I don't want them to love me," Heathcliff grumbled. "Before you came along, my idea of a perfect Christmas was eating jam toast alone in my room."

"Fine. *I* want the village to love you again. Or at least find you mildly tolerable. And this is the best way to do it."

"I bet Morrie left the oven on. I'll just pop back to the shop and check—"

"Nope." I shoved him into the room. Heathcliff wheeled his arms, trying to keep his balance. He whirled around, facing the audience of parents and children. His abrupt and un-Santa-like entrance stunned them into silence.

Or maybe their silence was because even though I'd warned the parents in advance, no one could quite prepare for the visual feast that was all 120kgs of Heathcliff Earnshaw bedecked in a bright-red Santa Claus costume.

"Ho," he said, in a tone one might use if they were about to head to the gallows.

I gestured at him. *More*, I mouthed.

Heathcliff glowered at me, then turned back to his rapt audience. "Hohoho," he added with a despondent sigh.

"Let's give Santa a big round of applause!" Morrie appeared from the size of the stage, wearing… *well*. He'd taken one look at the costume-store elf costume I bought him, declared no polyester would ever touch his skin, and had something sent up from London that was… well, it clung in *all* the right places. I'd noticed all the mums and quite a few of the dads checking him out.

Scattered applause rose from the gathered children. A few confused smiles broke out. "Why does Santa look so grumpy?" One boy asked.

"Because his lazy good-for-nothing elf hasn't brought Santa his Scotch," Heathcliff growled.

"Now, now, Santa," Morrie tsked, reaching for the pillow Heathcliff had stuffed under his red jacket and giving it a friendly pat. "We all know you're on a juice fast this Christmas. Your doctor said you need to lose some of this excess cookie weight. So no alcohol, and a strictly low-carb diet."

The children giggled. Heathcliff turned an even darker shade of *I'm-going-to-murder-you*.

I picked my way toward the back of the youth center, watching two of my boyfriends entertain a horde of kids while boyfriend number three croaked his approval from the rafters. My heart swelled to three times its size.

I found Mum with Mrs. Ellis and Jonie, manning a table laden down with Christmas treats donated by the village. Last night, we'd spent hours going around all the tables at the pub telling the story of what had happened and asking people to donate for the kids as well as to the animal charity tree. Argleton had really come through for us – kids and parents who often had nothing to eat were gorging themselves on fruit mince pies, trifle, chocolate fudge, Florentine biscuits, and leftover cuts of meat and piles of roast potatoes thanks to Richard at the Rose & Wimple. We'd invited everyone in the village to show up for the party, and it looked like most of them had shown up. Tabitha looked amazing in a red sequined dress and Elizabeth's black stone earrings as she greeted guests at the door. Even Roland crept around the room, snapping pictures for a new, "wholesome" version of the calendar.

Beaming with pride and joy, I loaded up a plate of treats for me and Quoth and settled in to watch the show.

"Who's first?" Morrie clapped his hands in glee as he herded the children toward Heathcliff's throne. "Come on, don't be shy! No need to crowd, you'll all get your turn. Santa is going to be here all day." His maniacal grin proved he was taking way too much pleasure in this.

Oh Morrie, don't ever change.

"Look at Heathcliff," Mum commented as she helped Earl Larson choose from the giant pyramid of Yorkshire puddings. Early slipped a piece of roast beef to the kitten perched on his shoulder, who mewed with pleasure."I never knew he was so civic-minded. He even looks like he's enjoying himself."

"I wouldn't go that far," I grinned. "But he does make a great Santa Claus. I wonder if we can convince him to do this every year?"

"I said no handing out caramels!" Heathcliff yelled at Morrie from his throne as a small girl clambered up on his lap with a handful of candies. "They'll get sticky fingers all over the presents and—"

"Don't listen to Santa, kids." Morrie shoved two more children toward him. Cameras flashed like lightning strikes as the parents recorded every moment of Heathcliff's ordeal. "Free caramels for all. Here, have a handful while you wait your turn."

"Croak." Quoth sighed as he settled on my shoulder. I nuzzled his head, watching in part-horror, part-joy as Heathcliff dumped a bowl of caramels down the back of Morrie's elf leggings.

Ah, Christmas. The most wonderful time of the year.

Correction. If your name is Mina Wilde, and you're an almost-blind punk rock bookseller with three boyfriends who were plucked straight from your favorite literary masterpieces and a crazy mother who wants to marry you off to the Napoleon of Crime, and you live in a picturesque village that must be the murder capital of England, in a magical bookshop with a room that skips around in time, then Christmas isn't just wonderful.

It's magic.

THE END

Morrie's been arrested on suspicion of murder. Mina knows the Napoleon of Crime is innocent, but how can she prove her favorite con-artist is being stitched-up? Find out in book 5 of the Nevermore Bookshop Mysteries, *Prose and Cons.*

Can't get enough of Mina and her boys? Read a free alternative scene from Quoth's point-of-view along with other bonus scenes and extra stories when you sign up for the Steffanie Holmes newsletter.

FROM THE AUTHOR

Ah, Christmas. The most wonderful time of the year.

I live in New Zealand, so the notion of a snowy, snuggly Christmas is completely foreign to me. Growing up, Christmas always meant presents in the morning, a BBQ or roast for lunch, and then off to the beach for swimming and sandcastle competitions. (My sister and I won once for our 'Homer Simpson Asleep On The Couch' sandcastle, complete with beer cans we found lying around on the beach.)

Christmas to me has always meant eating too much chocolate, and staying up late on Christmas Eve putting the last touches on homemade presents. It means seeing my niece and nephew excitedly ripping into their gifts. It means my husband giving me a gift at least two weeks early because he can't stand waiting another moment to see my reaction. It means forcing my cats to wear adorable little Santa hats while they try to dial an animal rights activist without opposable thumbs.

It means eating ALL the roast potatoes.

I hope you, dear reader, have a wonderful celebration surrounded by family and friends – no matter where you are or what cultural traditions you embrace. I hope that if the holiday season is a tough time of year for you – as it is for many – that you can find support and comfort and joy in the small things. A mug of hot chocolate. A good book. A hug from a friend.

If you need something to read over the holidays, I've got you covered. Check out my Briarwood Witches series – it's complete at 5 books, so that's 400,000+ words about a science nerd heroine who inherits a real English castle complete with great hall, turrets, and 5 hot English/Irish tenants. She also inherits some magical powers she can't control (also, there is MM). Grab the collection with a bonus scene. Turn the page for a teaser.

For something a little darker, try *Shunned*, book 1 of my Kings of Miskatonic Prep series. HP Lovecraft meets *Cruel Intentions* in a dark paranormal reverse harem bully romance about three broken bad boys and the girl who stood her ground. This is my most popular release EVER and readers are calling it, "The biggest mindfuck of 2019" so if you haven't read it already, I suggest you give it a try!

I've got lots of new books releasing soon, as well as some special surprises. Join my Facebook group Books That Bite or follow my Instagram to see more.

I'd like to thank my amazing family of writer buddies – aka, the Professional Perverts – for being by my side during an amazing year. Thanks Bri, Katya, Elaina, Kit, Jamie, and Emma for all the laughs and love.

And a big snuggly Christmas hug to my cantankerous drummer husband, who beta read this book and laughed the whole way through.

Until next time!

Steffanie

Dear Fae,

Don't even THINK about attacking my castle.

This science geek witch and her four magic-wielding men are about to get medieval on your ass.

I'm Maeve Crawford. For years I've had my future mathematically calculated down to the last detail; Leave my podunk Arizona town, graduate MIT, get into the space program, be the first woman on Mars, get a cat (not necessarily in this order).

Then fairies killed my parents and shot the whole plan to hell.

I've inherited a real, honest-to-goodness English castle – complete with turrets, ramparts, and four gorgeous male tenants, who I'm totally *not* in love with.

Not at all.

It would be crazy to fall for four guys at once, even though they're totally gorgeous and amazing and wonderful and kind.

But not as crazy as finding out I'm a witch. A week ago, I didn't even believe magic existed, and now I'm up to my ears in spells and prophetic dreams and messages from the dead.

When we're together – and I'm talking in the Biblical sense – the five of us wield a powerful magic that can banish the fae forever. They intend to stop us by killing us all.

I can't science my way out of this mess.

Forget NASA, it's going to take all my smarts just to survive Briarwood Castle.

The Castle of Earth and Embers is the first in a brand new steamy reverse harem romance by *USA Today* bestselling author, Steffanie Holmes. This full-length book glitters with love, heartache, hope, grief, dark magic, fairy trickery, steamy scenes, British slang, meat pies, second chances, and the healing powers of a good cup of tea. Read on only if you believe one just isn't enough.

Available from Amazon and in KU.

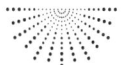

*R*owan showed Maeve around the kitchen, pointing out the spice racks and explaining his stupidly complicated fridge-stacking system. Maeve listened attentively, and she didn't laugh or poke fun of any of Rowan's OCD tendencies. The tension slipped from his shoulders. She was affecting even him.

"What are you making here?" Maeve peered into the baskets of produce and empty preserving jars on the island.

Rowan's face reddened and his shoulders hunched back up again. I winced. That didn't last long. Maeve looked at Rowan's face as his jaw locked. He stared at his feet and twirled the end of a dreadlock around his finger.

"Rowan, is something wrong?" Maeve's voice tightened with concern. She reached out a hand to him, but he stepped back, leaving her arm hanging in the air. The awkward tension in the air ratcheted up a notch.

Time to save this situation. I stepped forward and grabbed Maeve's arm, doing my best to ignore the tingle of energy that shot through me when our skin touched. I'd have to get used to ignoring it. I dragged her across the room.

"This is really cool," I said, opening a door at the back of the kitchen to reveal a narrow staircase. "This was installed when the castle was a grand stately home so the servants could rush meals up to the bedrooms without being seen in the main part of the house. It comes up near the staircase that goes up to your bedroom, so it's a good shortcut down to the kitchen if you fancy a nightcap."

"Duly noted." Maeve sashayed across the room and peered up the narrow staircase. "Are the bedrooms upstairs? Can I see?"

At the word *bedroom* passing through her red, pursed lips, my cock tightened in protest. *Don't think about it.* But that was like telling Obelix – the pudgy castle cat – not to think about all the delicious birds sitting in the tree outside the window.

"Sure." I gestured to the staircase. "After you."

Maeve started up the narrow steps, her gorgeous arse hovering inches from my face. I made to follow her, but something heavy slammed into my side, knocking me against the wall. I cursed as my elbow scraped against the rough stone of the wall.

"Sorry mate," Flynn flashed me his devil's grin as he leapt past me and followed Maeve up the stairs. "I didn't see you there."

"I believe you," I mumbled as I followed them up. "Millions wouldn't."

At the top of the stairs, Maeve pressed her hands against the wood panel. "How do you get this open?"

Flynn tried to reach around her to unlock the clasp at the top of the door, but this time, I beat him to it. As I reached around Maeve, she turned slightly to press her back against the wall and her breasts brushed against my shirt, setting off a fire beneath my skin.

Her lips formed an O of surprise, and I couldn't help but mentally fill in that O with the shaft of my cock. I blinked, trying to stop thinking about her like that, trying to remember that it was the magic making me into this *animal*.

The air between us thinned, and an invisible force drew my

body forward, my arm brushing hers. A few inches more, and my lips would be pressed against hers—

No. You can't do this. You can't encourage her to choose you.

"Well, isn't this intimate?" Flynn shimmied his way through the gap so that he had his back against the opposite wall, his hands falling against Maeve's hips. If he wanted, he could slide her back so her arse rubbed against his cock, and even though that was totally cheating, I wouldn't even blame him. I was cheating just as bad – my face in hers, my eyes begging for her touch. All I'd have to do was lean forward, press my lips to hers, and it would all be over…

Want to find out what happens next – Start The Briarwood Witches series today.

Art of Temptation (Alex & Ryan)

The Man in Black (Elinor & Eric)

Watcher (Belinda & Cole)

Reaper (Belinda & Cole)

Wolves of Crookshollow series

Digging the Wolf (Anna & Luke)

Writing the Wolf (Rosa & Caleb)

Inking the Wolf (Bianca & Robbie)

Wedding the Wolf (Willow & Irvine)

Fallen Sorcery Fae (shared world)

Hollow

Witches of the Woods

Witch Hunter

Coven

The Curse (coming in 2019)

Want to be informed when the next Steffanie Holmes paranormal romance story goes live? Sign up for the newsletter at www.steffanieholmes.com/newsletter to get the scoop, and score a free collection of bonus scenes and stories to enjoy!

ABOUT THE AUTHOR

Steffanie Holmes is the author of steamy historical and paranormal romance. Her books feature clever, witty heroines, wild shifters, cunning witches and alpha males who *always* get what they want.

Before becoming a writer, Steffanie worked as an archaeologist and museum curator. She loves to explore historical settings and ancient conceptions of love and possession. From Dark Age Europe to crumbling gothic estates, Steffanie is fascinated with how love can blossom between the most unlikely characters. She also writes dark fantasy / science fiction under S. C. Green.

Steffanie lives in New Zealand with her husband and a horde of cantankerous cats.

STEFFANIE HOLMES VIP LIST

Can't get enough of Mina and her boys? Read a free alternative scene from Quoth's point-of-view along with other bonus scenes and extra stories when you sign up for the Steffanie Holmes newsletter.

Come hang with Steffanie
www.steffanieholmes.com
hello@steffanieholmes.com

Printed in Great Britain
by Amazon

45696479R00085